Dear Kate–

Dear Dad,

ALSO BY THE AUTHOR

The Isle across Acheron

The Slip through Time

Denali Majesto's

Dear Kate—Dear Dad,

Dear Kate—Dear Dad,

Paperback edition first published in 2024

Title also available as a Kindle eBook.

Cover Design: J. Alder Buckthorne
Interior Design: Ansel Muir

Requests for information should be addressed to Chelsey Hanel via email at chelsey@denalimajesto.com.

Hardcover ISBN: 979-8-9928038-2-2

To inquire further or learn more about the library of Denali Majesto, please visit www.denalimajesto.com.

In deep thanks to my wife for following me across the world, to my children for reminding me how much impact I can have on people, and to all my ambassadors and friends who have worked tirelessly to build my dream.

---------- ONE ----------

It Begins with a Letter

August 19th, 2003

Dear Kate—

First things first: Happy birthday!

Second things second: Sorry I haven't bought you a present in the past couple decades. Does that make me a bad dad? If so, I'll try to make up for my failure now.

Though I wrote it many years ago, I asked your mom to give you this letter on your twenty-first birthday. I hope you didn't drink too much before reading it, because these are some of the most important words I've ever written. And, trust me, I've written a lot. However, since your first day of legal drinking also coincides with Jesus' 2,022nd birthday, I'm not holding out much hope. The world is observing its holidays, and I suppose it's only fair that you celebrate with everyone around you—booze included!

I wish to the stars that I could be there in person, Kate, handing you this letter myself, but life maps out different plans than ours. I now know it's impossible that I will be with you. That's just how things go sometimes. So, when life takes a crap all over your original plans, what can you do but create new ones? That's why I wrote this letter.

Fingers crossed that life is all pooped out.

Obviously, a few years have passed since you last heard from me. In fact, the last time you saw me, you would have been too young to remember. In order to atone for my absence, I have been beaver busy planning something spectacular for your twenty-first birthday. I hope my gift will not only inspire you and excite you, but that through it you might somehow feel connected to me again. I want to open up and lay bare a few chambers of my heart you never had the chance to experience.

You likely already know that I loved to travel. I spent most of my early twenties using my hard-earned paychecks to explore as much of our beautiful planet as I could. From the southernmost reaches of the Americas to the blast-freezer chill beyond the Arctic Circle, from the cracked-rust deserts of Australia to the high Sierras of California, I sought to soak up every sight and sound and scent this world could offer me. It became my undying passion, my purpose. In fact, I loved marauding about this planet so much, I eventually made a successful career out of it. As a travel writer and photographer, the globe was my office, airplane and train seats my desk chairs. It was a life I loved deeply.

The only force in heaven or earth which could have ended my nomadic existence was your mother. And, as I'm sure you're well aware, she is one damn powerful force. That's why I ultimately did settle down. Here in Colorado, we built a life together. I became a husband, a homeowner, a desk jockey editor. Most importantly, I became your dad.

I never once looked back. But, as your father, I did look forward to the day when you would be all grown up, and I'd have the chance to show you all those places dotted around our marbled globe that I so treasured. Sadly, I never got the chance.

This, then, is my birthday gift for you: to see and hear and touch just a few. I can't take you to *all* my favorites, so *some* will have to suffice. If even an ounce of my blood flows through your veins, I have no doubt you will love them too.

Before you start daydreaming about all the places *you've* always wanted to visit, you'd best stop, because those decisions were already made ... by me! I suppose you could think of this as a grand, global scavenger hunt. At each location I send you, you will find a letter from me. Those letters will provide you with instructions for the next leg of your journey. More importantly, each one contains a small piece of my heart's puzzle. As you assemble those pieces, I hope you might finally have a clear picture of my deepest reflections on you. All the pain. All the regret. All the joy. And, especially, all the love.

If you're wondering how you will pay for everything, fear not! The Father provideth. Long story short, I've made some sizeable investments in your name. They should be plenty to cover your travel expenses (and maybe a little left over to go toward college tuition or a house or the casinos in Black Hawk). Your mom has all the information required to access that account.

I also have two bonus gifts to accompany you on your travels. The first is a large, blank, leatherbound journal, identical to the ones I've used for years. I know this request might sound a little stupid—illogical, at least—but could you write to me in it? Keep me posted about your progress, as well as any thoughts or stories you want to share with your old man? The romantic in me imagines that, in this way, I might feel connected to you too.

The second bonus gift is my travel backpack, complete with all my favorite supplies. For nearly two decades, before your mom entered the picture, this pack was my best friend as I traveled the globe. Whether for work or vacation, I was never far from it. Inside you'll find my sleeping bag, tent, first aid kit (you'll want to restock the expired stuff… ibuprofen might turn into rat poison after twenty years), favorite Buck knives, a handheld GPS, my Polaroid camera, and an assortment of other camping/traveling paraphernalia. Take care of them, and they'll take care of you. Each item might come in handy at some point, but the GPS could be absolutely pivotal, *so don't lose it*.

That's all … for now. Happy birthday, and merry Christmas! Best of luck to you, my Kate, and enjoy the thrill of your journey!

I love you now and always,
Dad

Admittedly, the location of the first letter might sound a little underwhelming, especially after all this buildup. But don't worry! Some of the following letters will be so challenging to find, I'm actually a little worried you might not succeed on your own. If that does happen, talk to your mother. She's generally a helpful hand.

Now, without further ado—drumroll, please—you will find my next letter at your grandparents' mountain home. I'm sure you know the place. On their front porch, overlooking the frozen stream and snow-blanketed valley, is a tired pine cabinet already sagging with age. Inside it you will find a locked cash box.

The key to that cash box is the one you discovered when you opened this envelope. There you will find my next letter, as well as instructions for the next leg of your journey.

Do me a favor, will you? If the old rocking chair is still on the porch, sit there to read the letter. Once you've done so, I think you'll understand why.

It's pivotal that you begin this scavenger hunt right away during these winter months. If I planned everything out correctly, it'll mean you're on your holiday hiatus between college semesters. Use your winter break wisely, and I have no doubts you'll be able to finish the first few legs of the journey.

Needless to say, time is of the essence, so get moving right away, Cuddles!

December 25, 2022

Dear Dada,

Mom told me that's what I always called you—Dada—all the way from my first half-birthday until you were gone. Now that I'm an old lady (21 sounds super ancient to me), I guess I can finally drop the baby name and start calling you "Dad" like a normal person.

Except for the memories Mom shares with me, I don't know much about you. I have no recollections of my own. Not a single image. Not even one lonely, wistful whiff of my young life with you. It's as if there is a black hole, a blank space, in the *Dad* category of my childhood memories. Since talking about you was always so difficult for Mom, I learned not to ask about you too often. Even now, after so much time has passed, I know depressingly little about who my father was. Here's the list of what I do know:

~ I know your name was Isaac.

~ I know your favorite nickname for me was "Cuddles." You confirmed that at the end of your letter.

~ I know both your parents died in their forties.

~ I know you loved Mom. I can see so in your eyes whenever I look at your wedding picture.

~ I know you liked to drink beer, and that sometimes you liked to drink a little too much. (Uncle Ben shared that fun fact ... not Mom!)

~ I know I don't look anything like you. Your brown hair and dark eyes vs. my blond hair and blue eyes ... Are you sure you were really my dad? What did your mail man look like nine months before I was born?

- ~ I know I have your "slightly inappropriate brand of humor." (Mom's words, not mine.)
- ~ I know what your singing voice sounded like. Mom let me listen to a song you once recorded for her before an extended assignment overseas. Not too shabby!
- ~ I know you hated clichés. Mom tells me so whenever I use one. Don't worry, I'll try to avoid them like the plague whenever I write to you.
- ~ I know you liked going to the casino with Grandma and Grandpa. (Beer and gambling ... how many vices did you have? Is there, like, a twenty-year-old stash of cocaine squirreled away in one of our vents?)
- ~ I know how much you loved to travel.
- ~ And I know you died when I was only 21 months old.

As for me, I can't stand the taste of beer, my singing voice sounds like a dying monkey, I've never been to a casino, and the extent of my traveling ranges from California to Wyoming. We did go to Disney in Florida once, but I don't think the Epcot countries count as "traveling."

I guess I do know one more thing: that I inherited your writing gene. That's probably why I'm still awake at 11:03 on Christmas night after way too many Fireball shots with Mom and her gigantic, crazy-ass family.

An hour ago, when the full regiment of uncles, aunts, and cousins finally filed out our front door, Mom called me up to her room and handed me a key.

"It opens the rolltop desk," she explained, quickly and in subdued tones.

For as long as I can remember, that hundred-pound hunk of wood in her bedroom corner has existed as taboo territory. My whole life, every drawer has been locked tight, never opened. She denied my requests to look inside so many times that I was only seven when I gave up asking. I always realized its contents must have something to do with you. I just never knew what, exactly.

My stomach began turning somersaults as I inserted and turned the key. I tried to tell myself it was the Fireball. Really, though, I was afraid of disappointment. Long had my wild imagination dreamed of the mysteries which might live inside the desk, and I didn't want reality to let me down. The lid, reluctant after too many years of disuse, required some gentle coaxing as I rolled it back. I expected to find a clutter of papers and planners and photos inside, the rusted-out remains of your professional life, but the flat surface of the desk was mostly empty. Only two items sat there, one on top of the other. A plain, dark book beneath an envelope already yellowing with age.

Written on the envelope's tired face was a simple message: *For Kate, on Her 21st Birthday.*

"Your dad wrote it for you," Mom said, trying to keep her emotions stable, "not long before he died. It's been waiting in here ever since."

I tried to say something but couldn't. My voice was broken. Struck dumb, I picked up your letter and the book underneath.

"He also wanted you to have that journal," said Mom. She ran her hand up and down my back, then squeezed me close to her side and whispered, "Good night. Happy reading, Little Love."

She started to turn away before whipping back around. "Oh! I almost forgot!"

She slid open a small drawer just above the desk's writing surface and produced from within a thin, pocket-sized booklet. Emblazoned in gold on its front cover were the words: *PASSPORT – UNITED STATES OF AMERICA.*

"It may have been slightly illegal," she said, handing me my first passport, "but I took the liberty of filling out and signing all the paperwork to get you this."

"What do I need a passport for?" I asked. "What's going on?"

"It'll make sense once you read the letter," came her cryptic reply. "And now, for the last time, goodnight, sweetheart."

Still unable to believe what I was holding, I went to my room. I sat on my bed. I hugged my ancient, blue stuffed horse close to my chest with one hand as your letter trembled in the other. I spent the next fifteen minutes ugly-crying, reading and rereading the words my dead dad left me so long ago.

When I could read no more, I traded your letter for the leatherbound journal. (Sounds so sophisticated!) Now I'm writing to you, as requested, and trying not to ugly-cry for a fourth time.

I have to admit, Dad, this came from way outta left field. Actually, this came from the parking lot outside the stadium walls a hundred feet *past* left field. You don't get me a present for twenty years, and then this is dropped in my lap? What the hell! I think you owe me some dolls, and play houses, and a beat-up sixteenth-birthday car before throwing anything this huge at me. You just took the phrase "birthday surprise" to a whole new freaking level!

Doing what you're asking me to do, dropping everything for an unplanned trip around the world, taking a break from a few weeks of life ... sounds like a bit much, doesn't it? For starters, my boyfriend would be super crabby about it. (You actually met him when he was a toddler. He's Tom and Cheryl Murphy's son, Andrew. They were close friends of the Goodings. Getting off-track. Sorry.) Tomorrow I'm supposed to drive up to Cheyenne to meet his extended family and stay at his parents' house until New Year's. My best friend Emma would also be disappointed, because we've had tickets to go to the Broncos game on New Year's Day for the last five months. She would forgive me for that, but I don't know if I would ever forgive *myself* for missing out. Then, of course, I have to consider the very real possibility that my boss will fire me if I'm not back in my Chili's uniform on January 2. And none of this yet mentions the fact that I was looking forward to, like, eight seconds of relaxation before starting my second semester at the University of Wyoming. Right now I'm having a teeeeensy bit of trouble envisioning how an impromptu, worldwide journey fits into those plans.

So here's the deal I'm gonna make with you: I'm spending tomorrow with Andrew's family. I feel I at least owe him that much. The next morning I'll get up early, drive to Grandpa's (Grandma died a few years ago, but I'm sure you know that ... Hi, Grandma!), find your next letter, and be back at Andrew's by late afternoon. Then I will think about when, or *if,* I can do the rest. Sound good?

I'll take your silence as a "yes."

OK. Time for some rest. I'm supposed to leave at eight o'clock tomorrow morning, and I have no small amount of liquor to sleep off.

Love, your (slightly inebriated) little girl,
Kate

P.S. Sorry if that sounded a little harsh or ungrateful. It's just ... *wow* this is a lot to take in right now! I'll try to be nicer in the future. I promise!

October 23rd, 2002

Dear Kate—

I've always found the moon funny. Not funny in the "haha" way. Funny in the sense that you can look at it, observing it for years and years, and yet never quite feel like you understand it. I can't tell you how many nights I myself have spent staring at it. And it doesn't matter which hemisphere you're in, or whether you're north or south of the equator; sometimes you see more of it, and sometimes less, but the portion we *can* see always stays the same. You can gaze up at the moon for a hundred years, or a thousand, and you will never see anything new.

What I find strangest about our moon, though, is that you never see its other half. Whenever it is bright and round we call it a *full* moon, but even a full moon is truly only ever *half* the moon. No matter what, its dark side remains dark. For those of us obligated to the gravity of this little sphere, the moon's backside remains a mystery, a cosmic riddle, an enigma about which we can only dream and daydream.

Since the first time your mother brought me here, to your grandparents' mountain home, I have loved staring up a quarter million miles through atmosphere and space to admire that lunar landscape from this porch. Long after everyone else goes to sleep, I will sit quietly, listening as the melodies of our world and the universe raise their voices in harmony with one another. Here I've always felt safe, protected, as if every empyreal force were standing guard over me.

You can't possibly remember, but on this porch is where I sat with you every night for two straight weeks. You were only a month old back then. Your mom and I, like most brand new parents, struggled when you were born. Some nights we were so exhausted and sleep deprived, we were tempted to climb into a full bathtub hugging a plugged-in toaster. Unless someone—anyone—were holding you, you would cry and fuss and scream tirelessly until someone picked you up. Your grandma and grandpa very graciously invited us up here so they could help out and we might actually get some sleep. (I contacted the Catholic Church to have your grandparents sainted, but for some reason they denied my request. They must be ageists.)

Somehow I still ended up holding you late into the night. I was tired, but I didn't mind because—and this couldn't be more cliché if the song "Butterfly Kisses" were playing in the background—from the moment I heard your first cry in the hospital, I was madly in love with you. So the two of us would come out here into the bitter cold, you wrapped up warm as a malaria-stricken Florida sunbather in your blankets, and we would sit on the tall, oak rocking chair. Back and forth, back and forth we would sway, a mighty ship on the waves with the most precious cargo in its hold. Eventually, the cold would get to me—it *was* February up in the mountains, after all—and I would retreat to the sofa in front of the glowing fireplace. That's where I invariably fell asleep every night, you in my arms, until your grandma stole you away and sent me to bed.

One of those nights I remember as clear as the frosted night sky. You lay in my arms as the mighty arm of the Milky Way cradled us both from overhead. The rocker creaked its back-and-forth rhythm. The moon was crescent, as curved and slender as a Soviet sickle. Even though it was so small, the light reflected off its shy face was bright enough to illuminate the gaping valley below. The icy waters of the stream became a ribbon of frosted silver, the grass and the trees on the mountainsides a mercurial quilt.

I stared down at your sleeping face. So little of you I had seen! Such a tiny fraction of your life had come and gone. And yet you lit up every corner of my world, dispelled every shadow in my heart. I knew then that my life was finally complete, that you had filled a hole inside me I didn't even know existed.

I never expected to know you fully, just as we earthbound mortals will never fully know our moon. We aren't meant to see every part of the people around us, not even the ones we know and love best. But I did expect to see more. I looked forward to the day when I would behold you, the full moon, the full Kate, in as much detail and beauty and light as might be permitted for one man to see.

Life, though, can have very different plans than our own. Sometimes beautiful. Other times unpredictable and cruel.

You were three days shy of your second monthday when Dr. Gross gave me the results of my blood tests in his hushed, sympathetic tones. I meandered home, dazed, destroyed. I stood beside your crib while you napped and let my silent tears cascade to the floor.

That was the day I knew that the sliver was all I would ever get to see. You would wax into a quarter, a gibbous, a full moon.

But you would do it without me.

I admit, I felt sorry for myself. It was hard not to. In the end, though, I was thankful. My heart overflows with gratitude, even as I write this letter, because you're the young moon, the crescent sliver, who makes even the darkness in my life light up like the noonday sun. And when I do go gentle into that good night, it will be the radiance of your little life sending me off.

Thank you for your light, my Kate. Know that I never took it for granted.

Know that I never will.

I love you now and always,
Dad

Now your journey must grow harder. The time has come for you to leave the country, to wave goodbye to the continent. You'll want to pack a couple of your warmest, wooliest sweaters, because 69-degrees north is a bit nippy this time of year!

Your first task will be booking a flight to Tromsø, Norway. From there, rent a car and drive to the Jolly Orcas pub in a tiny town called Lyngenseidet. Ask for James or Callie Harden. They're an English couple who moved there and now specialize in northern lights tourism (and beer). They will be your guides for the next step in your journey.

Be safe. Be bold. And enjoy the adventure!

P.S. If the bar isn't there anymore, just ask around town for them. It's a small village, and I'm sure someone will know them!

P.P.S. If you don't do this now, in the dead of winter, you'll totally miss out on what I want you to see. So get your butt in gear!!!

December 27, 2022

Dear Dad,

That was a low damn blow, and you know it. I suppose I should have expected such a perfect degree of sentimental sap after reading your first letter. If your entire goal is making your little girl cry, you're two for two. Since I'm not particularly fond of tears, I would appreciate if you lightened the mood in your next letter.

I guess that's my subtle way of admitting that I'm going on the next leg of this scavenger hunt. After reading your letter, I'd feel too guilty *not* abandoning the rest of my winter break plans, hopping a plane to a foreign country, and tracking down a couple who, for all I know, may not even live in Norway anymore!

Actually, if I'm begrudgingly honest, this couldn't have come at a better time. Let's just say things have cooled with Andrew since Christmas night.

I met his extended family yesterday, like I told you. They seem great. Nice and fun and fairly normal.

But after all the aunts and uncles and cousins left his house, Andrew and I were sitting alone in front of the fireplace, and he started ... *talking*. Talking about how we were such a great fit together, about how well I get along with his family. You know, the kind of stuff intended to lead into a deeper conversation.

Andrew is a beat-around-the-bush kinda guy. But I ain't that kinda girl. So I asked, "Where are you digging with this?"

"The future." That's what he said. "*Our* future. What do you think?"

I chuckled, perhaps a bit dismissively, and replied, "I think it's way too late to talk about this."

"Really?" he countered. His gentle, green eyes showed a hint of confusion. "We've been dating since the end of summer. I don't think it's all that late."

"No, idiot, way too late at *night,*" I said. "The future will have to wait until tomorrow. I was up super late yesterday with that dad stuff, and I can hardly keep my eyes open anymore. I gotta get some sleep."

Andrew didn't protest. Truthfully, I didn't give him the time to do so, because I quickly kissed him goodnight, then stole through the darkness of the sprawling house to the guest room. If I'm being honest, though, I wasn't as terribly tired as I led Andrew to believe. Deep feelings have never been my forte, and sleep was an easy excuse to avoid them.

OK, that might be an understatement. The idea of talking about a future together with him totally freaked me out. Call me emotionally stunted or immature or whatever. I don't care. If I had to, I would have launched myself down a flight of stairs to get out of that conversation. I'm aware all I really did was kick the can down the road, but that's Future Kate's problem. She can deal with it.

Now that I think of it, there *is* someone safe I can share my deep, dark feelings with. But you have to pinky-promise not to tell anyone, Dad!

Here's what I think about Andrew's question ...

I think we've only been dating for five months. I think I'm a junior in college, and we're still too young to start talking seriously about marriage. He's a senior, though, which probably means he's freaking out about his future more than I am. I think Andrew is way more invested in me than I am in him, and last night was the proof in the pudding.

And I think I need to get the hell out of this country so I can clear my head.

Like I said before, your letter came at exactly the right time. You've gift-wrapped an exit for me and tied it with a Christmas bow. What perfecter excuse could a girl have than to obey her dead dad's final wishes? A few days outside the country, incommunicado, hunting for your next letter should buy me plenty of time to sort through my own head. Then, when I come home, my feelings and I will be good and ready to pick up that conversation with Andrew.

I guess buying a plane ticket is my next move. Halfway around the world, last minute, smack dab in the middle of the holidays ... Shouldn't be too expensive, right? Let's hope those investments you made twenty years ago did OK.

Andrew's gonna be so pissed. Well, maybe not *pissed,* but upset for sure. He's been looking forward to this week for a long time. I know I'm confused right now, but I still hope he and his family understand. I've put in too much work for them to hate me now.

OK. Time to make a phone call. This should be pleasant.

About as pleasant as donating a kidney.

Love, your (running-away-from-her-problems) little girl,
Kate

December 28, 2022

Dear Dad,

I already have a new love interest. When your old stockbroker showed me the account figures with my name on top, I just about kissed him.

Wonder if he's married ...

Now, should I pay off my student loans with this wad of cash? Or go on your crazy scavenger hunt? Decisions, decisions ...

You're lucky I believe in ghosts. I'm afraid you would haunt me if I chose Option #1, so I guess I'm going to Norway. North of the Arctic Circle. In freaking December.

Actually, you have my friend Emma to thank for the decision. After writing to you last night, I started panicking, so I called her this morning and told her to meet me at our go-to coffee shop. I knew she'd be free, because she doesn't work and her dad is out of town. Plus, Emma is the Yin to my Yang. I'm cynical, reserved, and can be a bit aloof, whereas she's a ray-of-sunshine personality bursting at the seams with bubbly joy and unquenchable optimism, traits I've always found strange considering her awful home life. She's like a daisy poking up through the cracks of apocalyptic rubble. I can always count on her to balance out my craziness, and vice versa.

"I don't know what I should do," I told her, the moment she flopped down next to me on our favorite sofa. This quiet corner near the back of the café always provides a fitting venue for our heart-to-heart chats about life.

"Don't know what to do about what? Andrew?" she asked, as I handed her the steaming Americano in my right hand. "Go easy on him. Boys are idiots when they don't feel like they're in control of anything. It's science."

I laughed, pulling my own coffee cup away from my lips so I wouldn't spill on myself.

"No, not Andrew," I said. "Well, maybe a little bit Andrew. But mostly I don't know what to do about my dad's trip."

"Seriously?" Emma retorted. The disgust painted in her smoky, Mediterranean eyes made me wonder if I should commit myself to an asylum. "What is there to think about?"

"I mean, am I crazy for doing this? Basically pressing *PAUSE* on my life to do this scavenger hunt thing?"

"Kate, you'd be crazy *not* to do this," Emma replied plainly.

"Why? It's not like I'm gonna disappoint my dad if I don't."

I must have pushed a button, because she crossed her olive-skinned arms and glared at me. I've seen her face burn with that Greek fire before, and I knew she was about to let me have it. I braced myself.

"You remember that vacation my dad took me on last summer? To that fancy resort in Punta Cana?"

I winced but said nothing. I'd already heard the story and knew exactly where she was taking us.

"I basically spent five days in paradise all by myself," she continued. "My dad sold it to me like it was gonna be this great father-daughter bonding trip. And he sure bonded with *somebody's* daughter. Multiple daughters, in fact. I barely saw him, because he was too busy screwing around with girls barely older than me. He'd flash a smile and the money in his wallet, and the next thing I knew, he'd be gone until morning."

"I know, I know," I placatingly replied, like a kid trying to avoid a lecture from her mother.

Emma ignored me. "I wish I could say it was a one-time thing. But that's what he's done on every trip we've taken since Mom disappeared. I make sure he books separate rooms now, because I was sick of waking up with a naked stranger in the bed next to mine."

She paused. Sipped. Collected her thoughts.

"Your dad has been dead a long time," she mused, "and he's *still* better than the one I've got. He spent the last months of his life putting this trip together for you. And, I love you, but you'd be a pretty shitty daughter if you let his dying work go to waste."

That's the nice thing about having a best friend you've known since second grade. They aren't afraid to call you to the carpet when you're being a dumbass. She tried to backpedal, of course, when I told her it would mean missing our Broncos game, but by that point it was too late. Her damage was irreversible.

So. I guess that's settled. The soonest reasonable flight I could find leaves in two days. When I called Andrew to tell him, he said wanted to come with me. I turned him down.

"Why not?" he asked.

I can tell I'm grinding down his patience.

"It's just something I have to do on my own," I answered. Of course, that wasn't enough for him.

"You're a pretty girl going to a strange country all by yourself," he argued. I imagined him with his hands shoved in his pockets and his shoulders hunched, just like he does every time he's irritated. "You don't know their culture, or their road signs, or their language. What if something happens to you? How would anyone even know?" Blah blah blah blah.

I tried to explain that I'm capable enough on my own, that practically everybody in Norway speaks English, and that my dead, demanding-to-a-psychopathic-degree dad is sending me there with about 22 total inches of Buck knife blade in my backpack. Still not enough for him. Not enough to ease his mind about what's *really* bothering him.

"What about New Year's Eve?" he asked next. "I mean—can't you wait a couple more days? I had something special planned."

For some reason, the image of a gigantic diamond ring started revolving before my eyes, and my stomach dropped like a skydiver in freefall. I guess I can't be certain he was planning a New Year's Eve proposal, but even the smallest possibility made me want to run to the nearest trash can and yak my guts out.

"I'm sorry," I said, perhaps a bit coldly, "but it'll have to wait. My dad planned something special for me twenty years ago. I think that means he has dibs."

Honestly, I'm a little surprised at myself. I thought I loved Andrew. I've even said it about a hundred times. But suddenly I'm not sure. The moment he started talking about the future, it was like our relationship was written in permanent marker or etched in stone. I don't know. Something just feels *off* between us. Or maybe I'm just scared, or maybe I'm not hardwired for commitment, or maybe I have issues with men because my daddy was never around when I was growing up. Thanks a lot!

Like I wrote yesterday, I need some space. I need to clear my head. How did you know all those years ago that this is the exact week I would need to leave the country? Were you some kind of secret prophet with fortune-telling powers? Or was it simply a father's intuition? Gotta keep your daughter safe from those good-for-nothing boys? If that was your plan all along, it was well played.

OK. I've got less than 48 hours before I need to be at the airport and about 48,000 things to do between now and then. Even though Mom is helping me as much as she can, my hands are still pretty full.

I'll check in again soon. Unless I freeze to death first.

Love, your (uncertain) little girl,
Kate

---------- TWO ----------

69° North

December 30, 2022

Dear Dad,

Well, here I am. On a plane. Right where you want me. Soaring 39,000 feet above the inkwell of the midnight Atlantic with about two hundred other passengers who all sound like they're Norwegian. Scandinavian, at least.

I've never felt so alone.

Last night, all that bravado I showed Andrew turned into cold feet, so I asked Mom to come with me. You know what she did? She laughed! She actually laughed right at my face and said, "Your dad has already sent me on enough adventures. Now it's your turn."

"But I'm nerrrrrvoooous," I replied, using a melodramatic, whiny voice she's always hated. "I have no idea what I'm doing."

Well, this was certainly a different girl than the one who had told off her boyfriend two days earlier. I'm not sure which is the real me. Probably the one with less balls.

Fortunately, Mom's pretty good at the whole "parent" thing. She *has* had double the learning experience with no dad around to pull his weight. Sometimes I think she could comfort a crocodile with a toothache.

"Wanna know a secret?" she said. "I never had any idea what I was doing either. Once, when your dad and I were still dating, he was off on an assignment in Thailand and convinced me to join him there for a week. When I landed in Bangkok, I expected he'd be at the airport waiting for me. Nope! He was about a hundred miles away, still deep in the jungle.

He'd arranged for one of his new friends—he always made new friends, no matter where he went—to pick me up and chauffeur me. Long story short, this friend had an ancient Volkswagen. Could've been the original VW, for all I know. Anyways, about an hour outside the city, it overheated and broke down. So this guy flagged down a total stranger, had a twenty second conversation that sounded like total gibberish in a language I didn't know a word of, and escorted me and my belongings into the back of this other man's pickup. My new gentleman took me miles and miles down a muddy jungle trail. I was pretty sure I was gonna die that afternoon. But I didn't. The road finally ended at a tiny resort made up of these rustic, beautiful huts. Everything was surrounded by an emerald, waterfall paradise. And that's where your dad was, shooting photos and writing about the celebration of Thailand's Water Festival in the rural jungles. I was so mad when I saw him. But then he flashed me that big, confident smile, and his eyes lit up, and I melted. In that moment, I realized I had never been in any real danger. Somehow your dad understood my limits, and he never pushed me past them. Right up *to* them every now and then, but never past. So I learned to trust him pretty quickly, even when he did ask some crazy things of me!"

"He never knew me, though," I countered. "He couldn't have known my limits when he set up this scavenger hunt. I was just a baby."

Mom chuckled, like I'd just uttered the stupidest phrase in all human history, and replied, "He was your dad. That counts for more than you might think."

Sure hope she's right! Either way, I suppose there's no backing down now. This flying tin can is already in the air, and for better or worse, I'm in it.

Andrew and I did leave things on a good note, by the way. Just before I went to the airport this morning, he showed up to see me off. He apologized for acting possessive and childish and wished me luck. Everyone has their flaws, I guess (except for me, of course), and Andrew is a genuinely good guy. I don't doubt that for a second. Maybe the last few days were nothing more than a rough patch we needed to work through.

Alright. Time to sleep before my five o'clock landing in Oslo. I've got about a four-hour layover there before the last leg north to Tromsø.

Love, your (apprehensive) little girl,
Kate

December 31, 2022

Dear Dad,

The past 24 hours have flown by faster than an intercontinental jet. Technically, the new year has already rolled in, crashing over me and the other partiers at the Jolly Orcas in a wave of champagne and cheers and kisses. (None of that last bit for me, although I did break the heart of some poor Viking boy who went in for it.)

A little before noon today, I landed in Tromsø. The line at the car-rental kiosk was short, and before long I was snug and warm in my rented Volvo, hands gripped like vices around the steering wheel as I tried to keep pace with the traffic racing across the snow-packed roads. In Colorado these Norsefolks would be called "maniacs," but based on the amount of honkage I heard from other drivers, apparently I'm the maniac here.

Despite my rocky start, the Volvo's GPS did a perfect job navigating me the two-hour-plus drive to Lyngenseidet. Once I cleared Tromsø, the city traffic thinned, even as the hunks of arctic snow basting my windshield thickened. I have the sinking sensation the poor visibility robbed me of some tremendous beauty as I cut around the curves of those fjords. Hopefully the weather will cooperate more graciously during my return voyage.

When I eventually crawled into the quaint, seaside town nestled against the west edge of the Lyngenfjord, I couldn't imagine what prompted you to choose this place over a billion others I passed on the way. As I slid to a stop on the leveled snowcrete (that's what I've decided to call the driving surfaces here) in front of the Jolly Orcas, I became even more skeptical.

Mom said you had an inappropriate sense of humor, and I began to wonder whether I was arriving at the punchline of a joke. ("What do you call a pod of killer whales laughing at a dumb daughter following her dead dad's letters to the deep Arctic in the middle of winter? JOLLY ORCAS! Ha ha!")

But the moment I stepped inside and into the warm glow of the empty bar, I understood. Outside it had the appearance of a dead, worn-out fisherman's shack. Within, however, was full of heart and life, even without any customers. From the piano standing in one of the far corners, to the cozy tables and booths; from the photographs of the fjord sleeping silently beneath the restless gaze of the northern lights, to the holly and Christmas wreaths and decorated tree, everything about the Jolly Orcas made me feel at home.

A salt-and-pepper-maned gentleman, tall and lean, emerged from the back room moments after I entered the bar. He was middle-aged and strikingly handsome, like the actor in every ED commercial ever made. The corners of his sea-green eyes crinkled above his taut and genuine smile.

For some reason he reminded me of you—your pictures, anyway.

"Afternoon, Miss!" he exclaimed cheerfully in his thick English accent. A large screwdriver (the tool, not the drink) was clutched in his hand. "What can I do for you?"

I cleared my throat, suddenly realizing how thirsty with nerves I was.

"I—uh—I'm looking for James Harden," I stammered. "Or Callie. Do you know how I can reach them?"

The barkeep set down his screwdriver and leaned forward. He rested his flannelled elbows on the bar top and eyed me suspiciously.

"I—I'm sorry. This is the Jolly Orcas, right?" I continued uneasily.

"You don't look a damned thing like him, you know that?" he responded.

The reply caught me off guard. "Like who?" I asked.

That friendly crow's-feet grin returned as he said, "Like your dad. It's who you are, yeah? You're Isaac's little girl." He chuckled. "Been waiting a long time for you."

Surprise left me as speechless as a Trappist monk.

"You have a place to stay the night? Here in town?"

Still dumbstruck, I lazily shook my head.

"Well, you're in luck," he continued. "We just had a cancellation on one of our rental cabins. Damn snow, see. But it means you'll have a quiet, reflective place to lodge."

"You're ... James? I'm assuming?" I asked, finally getting over my Little Mermaid Syndrome as I found my voice.

"Oh! Right! Sorry. Yeah, he's me, I'm him, and all that lot. Same James your dad knew, too. Which means *you're* Kate." He paused, shaking his head in disbelief, and muttered, "Bigger than I remember."

"He said you'd have a letter for me," I told him. I was unsure exactly how to broach the subject, so I opted for my time-tested direct and tactless route.

"True enough," he replied. "Well, Callie's got it, anyway. But we're under explicit instructions from your old man not to give it up until the right time, you see. What, with all the snow and it being New Year's Eve, I can tell you most assuredly, *now* is not the time. Barmen like me are much too busy, see."

"When, then?" I asked, a sense of something akin to panic rising in my chest. Maybe he doesn't understand, but I don't exactly have forever to spend on this intercontinental errand.

"When the time is right," came his cryptic reply. "For now, let's get you situated! Came by car, I assume?"

I nodded stupidly. "Good! Come on, then. I've got the biggest night of the year to finish getting ready for, and one of my damn taps still needs fixing. Follow me!"

James shouted a quick note of departure to someone named Anna in the kitchen, then beckoned me to come after him. He jumped into an old truck and was off before I could even start my engine. Against every instinct I have about driving in snow, I sped and caught up to him. We headed north for ten or fifteen minutes. I sensed, even amid the sunken clouds and snow, that we were skirting the approximate edge of the fjord, but was unsure where he was taking me and why. Eventually James turned off the main road and began crawling up a steep hill. The trusty Volvo kept pace with his winter-tired truck. Finally, near the hill's crest, we reached identical, quadruplet cabins.

James stopped at the first. I made like I was also going to stop, but he waved me on and yelled, "Next one up on the right! Park there!"

So I did. By the time I stepped out of the car, James had already trekked the short distance up the hill.

"Come on in," he beckoned, unlocking the front door and waving me inside.

The cabin was modern, simple, and perfect. A narrow flight of stairs next to the front door led to an A-framed loft. One side of the main level was claimed by a cozy pair of snug bedrooms and a washroom. An open-concept kitchen/dining room/living room occupied the rest. The cabin's most spectacular feature, however, was the floor-to-ceiling assembly of windows, which spanned the entire width of the cabin's north wall.

"On clear nights," James explained, "our guests have a front row seat to watch the northern lights. Splendid spectacle, if you've never seen them. Or even if you have! Not much chance they'll be out tonight with all the clouds and snow flyin'."

Turning away from the gabled wall of glass, I asked, "James, why did my dad send me here?"

He shrugged, flashed me that grin which could have charmed the pants off George Clooney, and said, "I don't know exactly, but I imagine it has something to do with the letter that's been sleeping in my desk drawer for the last two decades. Knowing your dad, he'll sort it out soon enough. But only when the time is right." Seeing the irritation on my face, he added, "Sorry! Isaac's orders! You get the letter when you get it. Now, let me help you unload your things. You'll stay here until it's time to go. If you'd like, Callie and I would be honored to have you at the Orcas tonight for our New Year's celebration."

"And I'd be honored to go!" I answered cheerily, mirroring his upbeat disposition.

Everything since then is a merry haze, due both to alcohol and a frenzied flurry of activity. I met auburn-haired, rosy-cheeked Callie—sweet as crème brulee iced with a snow cone—and they brought me back to the Jolly Orcas earlier this evening. They and I and three dozen other friends and customers gorged ourselves on creamed mushrooms and sausages with lingonberry jam. We drank spiced Christmas beers and aromatic aquavit and some sharp, syrupy stuff called gløgg. At midnight we popped champagne and further stuffed ourselves with a giant, Christmas tree-shaped dessert called Kransekake. Men and women toasted and kissed (expect for myself and that poor, blonde Norwegian fella) and left shortly after for their respective homes.

Callie brought me back here while James stayed to close down and lock up. She suggested I sleep on the sofa, not the bed, so I would be in the living room, facing the high windows, if the clouds broke and the aurora began pouring down on me.

That's where I am now, writing yet again to the long-gone dad I never got to know. Another year without you has come and gone. Ahead of me is a brand new one from which you will remain always absent.

It's strange, but until now I never felt cheated. According to TV shows and movies in which the main character grows up without one or both parents, I knew I should. They're the characters who are distant, wrestling with inner demons sunup to sundown, forced into all kinds of self-destructive decisions. But that was never me. I never held to some idea that my life was a tragedy and I its afflicted, woebegone protagonist. Attribute it to my awesome single mom or to DNA or to luck, but I was content. Maybe not every moment of every day, but the general pattern of my life was that of a happy, well-adjusted (if not slightly cynical) girl.

Tonight, though? After hearing James and Callie rave about you? Share stories in which you brought joy and adventure to their lives? It's hard not to feel cheated now. It's hard not to wonder how much fuller my already-brimming life might have been.

But the cards have been dealt. The die has been cast. Whatever cliché has already been clichéd. No good poker player complains about her hand, because she knows whining won't help.

She can only play that hand the best she is able.

Still, I have to ask: What other cards will you deal me before this is over? What do you have hiding up your sleeve? And, I wonder, what'll it do to the hand I was holding before this began?

Can't wait for the answers this New Year will bring!

Love, your (contemplative) little girl,
Kate

January 1, 2023

Dear Dad,

It was another gray day at 69-degrees north. James and Callie both took the day off. "Hangovers and bar work don't mix well" was the justification James gave. They have a little motorboat, so my English friends guided me on a tour of the fjord. It was freezing but definitely worth it! For two hours we skimmed along that watery valley, cradled between the ever-watching slopes of white mountains. Even though the peaks of the Lyngen Alps were draped in hoods of mist, the vision was enough to steal the living breath from my lungs.

The best part of the trip, however, happened during our return to the dock, when a whole pod of killer whales surfaced right alongside our boat. They showed off their aquatic dance routine, gave a few toothy grins, and then continued on their journey. Once they had gone, Callie told me some live to be almost a hundred in the wild.

It made me wonder ... did you perhaps see these same orcas? Did you gasp with awe when their misty geysers plumed alongside you? Reach out, breath locked in your chest, to touch one, while at the same time praying your hand wouldn't get ripped off?

I find that I'm starting to ask so many questions I'll never have answered. Unless, of course, you used those fortune-telling powers of yours to anticipate my inquiries when you wrote your letters. Speaking of which, I'm still waiting on your next one. And patience ain't a virtue I value highly. So ... chop-chop, Dada!

As long as plans don't change, James is hooking me up tomorrow with a dogsled operator he knows. Now *there's* something I never dreamed I'd do! I've already eaten a vast menu of new and exotic foods, and in the morning, I'll add powdery Norwegian snow and sled-dog fur to that list. Interesting things happen when you're on top of the world, I guess!

Anyway, just wanted to check in. I'm about to eat dinner with Callie and one of her friends. Speaking of new foods ... sounds like reindeer is on the menu. Don't hold it against me, Santa!

Love, your (frozen) little girl,
Kate

January 1st, 2003

(to be read beneath the northern lights)

Dear Kate—

Breathtaking, aren't they? The first time I watched their heavenly dance, I teared up. I don't know that I have ever experienced anything so magical. Not before. Not since. Streams of emerald and crimson and violet, intertwining, braiding as one, then peeling away to fade into nothingness. These are the northern lights, the *aurora borealis.*

They're the reason I sent you to Norway in the heart of winter. These months are when our world's upper latitudes dwell in darkness, yet this is also when the aurora springs into the prime of its life. No one, in my estimation, can truly claim they've lived until they have witnessed this ethereal waltz. The ghostly lights have a way of sparking fire within the soul. They fill a person's heart with the vibrant and truest colors of life.

The ancient Vikings called the aurora by a different name: *bivrost.* It's a combination of two Norse words. Translated literally, it means "shaking road." Those Norsemen of long ago believed the northern lights constituted a road, a bridge, between earth and heaven. The gods and spirits of the dead would travel across this road whenever the *bivrost* appeared in the night sky. Thus they remained connected to the life and people they had left behind at death, continuing to keep watch over those they loved.

As I traveled back and forth across the world, I came to realize something about every culture or religious grouping I met: they all have their ideas about what a person does after they die. For most cultures, these death stories included a similarity to that of the ancient Vikings: some type of connection through which the dead could keep watch over the living. Many countries in Central and South America celebrate the Day of the Dead, a festival during which the spirits of their ancestors can return to visit them. Western cultures like ours, godless though they've become, still largely cling to the idea that their deceased loved ones become guardian angels who protect them. In China, people venerate their long-gone ancestors, who continue to bless—or curse—them. I even remember an Indonesian island where people kept bodies of dead relatives in their homes, giving them three meals a day as if they still needed to eat!

Finally, I had to ask myself the question: What is it about death which makes humanity so uncomfortable? Which maybe even *terrifies* us? Perhaps the common explanation, our innate fear of the unknown, plays a part in this, but I've come to believe a much truer reason lies beneath.

It's the separation. Separation from the people, possessions, and activities we loved so much during our time on this earth. Quite simply, death means being somewhere they are not.

If I'm being honest, Kate, that is what I'm most afraid to face. Not the stopping of my heart. Not my final breath. Not the electrical impulses in my brain falling silent.

I'm afraid of being separated from you and your mom.

How will I no longer cuddle you in my arms at night before you go to bed? Or in the morning while you drink milk from your sippy cup and we watch *Blue's Clues* together? And how will I not hike with you bouncing in the kid-carrier on my back, as you point out every stream or lake or pond or puddle we come across and insistently cry out, "Bubbles! Water!"? How won't I watch your excited eyes grow into saucers every time you taste a novel food that you love? Or see a Micky Mouse anything? How will I no longer hold your hand as you zoom down a slide, or sit on the swing, or wobblily toddle across your kiddie pool in the backyard? How can I not hear your sweet little cries for "Mama" and "Dada" over your baby monitor in the middle of the night, and find a weird reassurance those whimpers mean you're still breathing one room away? How will I not tickle you? Wrestle with you on my bed? Fly you over my head like an airplane? Kiss you goodnight? Hug you before work? Read to you before bedtime? Sing softly as you fall asleep next to me?

These are the questions that plague me, which keep me tossing and turning at night. The death sentence already looms over my head. It isn't a question of *if* anymore, but *when* the grave will separate me from you.

Now, as I write this letter to you, I find myself pondering these northern lights, the *bivrost* of the Viking peoples. Over and over again, the same yearning desire plays upon my mind like a CD track on repeat.

Could there really be such a bridge? Certainly not one which will let me rejoin you on earth once I am gone. But could there be a bridge between heaven and earth which will let me see you? Watch over you? Show me who you are, and who you've become? So that, even though I'm gone, I might see more than that crescent moon of your infant years?

I guess I won't know the answer until I arrive at whatever lies beyond the grave. But know this, Cuddles: If there is any way I can watch over you, I am doing just that. In fact, I sent you to Norway in the dead of winter on the millionth percent, shot-in-the-dark chance that those Norsemen were correct in their beliefs about the afterlife.

By now you're probably half frozen to death. But do your old dad a final favor tonight. Look up once more at those dancing waves of light. Because if there is even the most infinitesimal possibility they *are* a bridge between heaven and earth, I would love nothing more than to gaze on the radiant face of my little girl one more time.

After all, nothing ever did make me happier than that.

I love you now and always,
Dad

I suppose this means it's time for me to send you on the next leg of your trip. As with Norway, it is rather imperative you do this during your winter months. I'm hoping you still have a slice of Christmas vacation left.

That's because I'm sending you … into summer! Right now you're in the high north, but in the far-flung parts of Chile and Argentina, deep in the southern wilds of Patagonia, summer has barely begun. There couldn't be a better time of year for a hike through one of South America's most famous national parks: Torres del Paine. Once there, go to the guard shack at the Torres campground (closest one below the famous mountain towers). That is where your next letter awaits you.

January 2, 2023

Dear Dad,

I keep thinking my conversations with Andrew couldn't possibly become any less pleasant, and then you serve that onto my plate? This afternoon Callie helped me research airfare and the general trip to these "Torres" in Chile, and it means a whole extra week away from home! Andrew's not the kind of guy to speak ill of others, especially the dead, but when we were video-chatting and I told him I'd be heading to South America next, I definitely heard him send some shockingly disrespectful slurs your direction. Can't say I entirely blame him. I don't know how many thousands of miles separate the top of the world from the bottom, but I *do* know I'm looking less than forward to covering them all during a day-and-a-half-long, airport-to-airplane relay. Definitely not your most courteous hour.

To get even with you, I decided to stick around for my dogsledding adventure today. James's friend Erik gave me the "extra-special grand tour." For a good chunk of the afternoon, we ripped across blinding white slopes of purest snow and wove through groves of evergreen and birch. The ride ended at a brilliant overlook of the whole Lyngen fjord, glittering like a billion diamonds in the pale Arctic glow.

I know I've been a bit snarky with you at times in my writing (I'm not the best "feelings" person in the world), but I'm about to open up. This is a big moment for me. Ready for it?

Thank you. Even if the rest of this trip sucks ass ... thank you for Norway and Lyngenseidet. Between the shimmer of the wrinkled sea, and the northern lights, and the New Year's party, and these ice-sculpted mountains, I can say with ironclad for-surety that I've never been anywhere half as beautiful. I now realize you knew exactly what you were doing when you decided to send me here.

I have a feeling you would've been a halfway decent dad when I was growing up.

It was quite the coincidence that you mentioned Bivrost in your letter. James and Callie had just explained that fun tidbit of Norse trivia about an hour before I read it.

"A bridge that connects the living with the dead," Callie mused over tea yesterday evening. "Some believe it entirely true, but even the unbelievers catch themselves wishing it were so. Then, when the aurora shines, both believer and unbeliever alike stare up at the sky and together experience a strong feeling of connection with someone they've lost."

Perhaps my own experience was due to the fact that I was reading your letter beneath their spectral glow. Maybe heaven itself swept me up into a more spiritual state of consciousness. Who knows. But in one of those fiery spins, I swear I saw your kind face beaming down on me.

OK. I better turn off the feelings faucet now, or God only knows what other mumbo jumbo will come pouring out. But I'm glad I have you as a sounding board. Maybe you don't remember, but you *are* dead. And that means you can't make me feel insecure about my feelings! (Or maybe prodding the areas of my worst insecurities is the plan for your next letter. I guess I'll find out soon enough.)

Love, your (mushy, gushy) little girl,
Kate

---------- THREE ----------

The Southern Wilds

January 4, 2023

Dear Dad,

Here are some more feelings.

I hate you.

I never got to shout those words at you in the throes of some childish, teenage tantrum, so I'm saying it now.

I. Hate. You.

Thirty-two hours. Thirty-two shitty-ass hours. That's how long I've been living this nightmare. It's amazing, and a little scary, how easily my hand inks these words onto the page: I hate you. I do.

Right now I'm somewhere over the mid-Atlantic, and, honestly, I'm praying both pilots die of a stroke. This plane going down might be the only thing that can put me out of my misery. Currently, I'm wedged between an overweight couple who apparently demanded aisle seats for the extra room. I, however, am convinced they simply didn't want to spend eight hours smelling each other. Overripe onions are sitting on one side of me and an entire bottle of cheap perfume on the other. I've been hitting the lavatory so often in my desperate attempts to escape them that the flight crew probably thinks I have some serious IBS.

This is a nightmare. If you weren't already dead, I'd kill you. Since that's not an option, I'm distracting myself by writing.

When I left Norway yesterday, James and Callie seemed disappointed to watch me go. The feeling was quite mutual. I enjoyed their company tremendously and understand why you entrusted them with your letter. I promised them I would come back soon, and I plan to make good on my word. They told me I'd always have a free place to stay, and Lyngenseidet is far too beautiful to keep absent for long. I might even think about applying for a bartending gig at the Jolly Orcas if my whole actuarial science major doesn't pan out.

To be clear, I still hate you. That's not going to change. At least not until I get off this plane and take a shower. But even though I hate you, I guess I owe you one for introducing me to Norway.

OK. I need to take a break from my role as the deli meat in this onion-and-perfume sandwich. Time to hit the head again.

Hate, your (miserable) little girl,
Kate

January 5, 2023

Dear Dad,

I have arrived safely in Punta Arenas, deep at the bottom of the inhabited world. After that hellish flight, I splurged and booked myself a fancy schmancy hotel room. When I sit outside on my balcony, the icy blue Straits of Magellan are only a stone's throw away. Further, far across the Straits, the green slopes of Tierra del Fuego slice upward from the sea.

Soon, I think I'll take a walk around this charming town to grab a bite. There's something called a *completo* the bellhop told me to try. From what I gather, it's essentially a Chilean hot dog. Not sure how much better it could be than an American hot dog, but why not give it a shot?

When in Rome! (Or Punta Arenas!)

Maybe I had too much time to think during the flight, but my last video chat with Andrew has been weighing on my mind. I reflected on how I've been treating him, and I haven't exactly been the best girlfriend. He's always been good to me, and he deserves more patience in return. I'm not saying I'm suddenly ready to marry the guy, but maybe I could share my thoughts and (ugh!) *feelings* about our relationship a bit more. Writing in this journal has been giving me tons of practice after all! Maybe I can graduate to expressing those feelings to the living by the time I return home.

Mom messaged me yesterday, so I need to reply before heading off again tomorrow. Nothing too crazy going on back home, she's just curious how the trip is going. She'll die of surprise when she finds out I'm in Patagonia now! (Though I hope she doesn't. I'm not cut out for life as an orphan.) I guess I should keep her a little more up-to-date of my travels. After all, if I get kidnaped and sold on the black market, how would anyone know where to begin the investigation?

That's all for now. Tomorrow I take a bus (more sitting for hours on end, yaaaaaay) to an even smaller town called Puerto Natales. The gateway to Torres del Paine. And to your next letter.

Love, your (recuperating) little girl,
Kate

January 6, 2023

Dear Dad,

The stretch of Patagonia between Punta Arenas and Puerto Natales is the embodiment of desolation. There are only a few small hamlets and gas stations along the route. Yet in the emptiness, there prevails an intimidating sort of loveliness. During the four-hour bus trip, my eyes feasted on infinite swaths of choked grasslands studded with ponds and lakes, each one an azure gem sparkling under the rich afternoon sun. Far to the north and west, the jagged teeth of the southern Andes rose up and nearer, the fangs of some planet-devouring beast about to feast. Willingly I rode toward those great and empty jaws, feeling further from home than ever before among that lonesome landscape.

When the bus finally arrived in Puerto Natales, I spoke to the elderly bus station attendant in my broken Spanish about connecting to the park right away. She simply chuckled and informed me that it was too late in the day to begin a trip to Torres del Paine. Noticing my concern about having no place to stay, she kindly called up one of the local youth hostels on my behalf. They had a vacancy, so I headed there straightaway.

The hostel is owned and operated by a vibrant young couple from New Zealand, Bret and Jezzi. It's their custom each evening to invite their guests out into their cozy, fenced garden area for fellowship, which is how I found myself nursing an intoxicating glass of Pinot Noir in their company.

Sometime during the course of our conversation, once the courage of the wine had loosened my lips, I asked, "How did you end up in Puerto Natales, so far from home?"

Bret surprised me as he threw back his head and laughed, like I'd just told him the funniest joke in the celebrated history of jokes. "Home?" he roared. "Home's not three inches away! From the moment Jezzi an' I first stepped off the bus here eight years ago, this's always been home. Home is wherever you feel most alive."

I don't know why I felt like sharing that detail with you. It seems pretty insignificant, even in the grand scheme of this single day. But it got me wondering if that's how you saw the world sometimes, as if "home" were all those scattered places, flung across the globe, which made your heart warm and vibrant and full.

That is, until Mom and I created a new home—a permanent one—for you.

It really is true what they say: Home is where the heart is! Platitudes aside, I find myself wondering where *home* really is for me, but I guess I can't spend too much time mulling the question tonight. I need to squeeze in one last shower before Torres del Paine! I have a hunch it might be a couple days before that opportunity presents itself again.

Love, your (musing) little girl,
Kate

January 7, 2023

Dear Dad,

When I told them why I had come to the guard cabin, the two rangers stationed at the Torres campground looked like I had just grown an arm from my forehead. They stood there, mouths hanging open like a pair of frogs trying to catch flies. Neither one said anything for at least fifteen seconds.

The younger and scragglier-bearded of the two rangers (whose name I discovered later to be Franco) finally managed to choke out a couple words. "You are ... real?" he asked, as disbelieving as if he were speaking with a unicorn or leprechaun or honest politician.

"Yeeeees? I think so?" I replied, taken aback by their taken-abackedness. "At least, last time I checked I was."

Franco exchanged a glance with his colleague, Paulo, a stocky fellow at least twice Franco's age and with half the hair. Paulo merely shrugged his beefy shoulders and said, in rather broken English, "She is ... now here. Give her the letter."

"When the other rangers hear about this ..." Franco muttered, flashing me a genuine grin of excitement.

He led the way into the cabin. Really, it was not much more than a hut with a desk, filing cabinets, and a loft, which I assume must house their beds and personal belongings. As if pulled there by a magnet, Franco confidently opened one of the filing cabinet's drawers and reached deep inside. It appeared as if he had done this hundreds of times before. When he withdrew his hand, he held an envelope, yellowed with age, pinched between his fingers.

Scrawled across the front was your unmistakable handwriting: *For Kate Jackson. Expect her between Winter 2023—Spring 2024. Tell her to read at the Torres.*

Franco handed me the envelope. My heart fluttered when I felt the stale paper crinkle in my hands.

"You and this letter," Franco said, his voice low and creamy smooth, "are something of a legend around here."

I stared at him, puzzled.

"Understand, please, that we have dreamed about the contents of this letter for years—some for almost two decades—ever since the mysterious man delivered it here," Franco explained. Motioning toward his partner, he added, "Paulo was here that day. Although I am sure he was a thinner and much handsomer version of this meatball!"

Ignoring Franco's comment, or perhaps not knowing enough English to recognize the other's jabs at him for what they were, Paulo stepped forward and started speaking in Spanish. He went on, uninterrupted, for over a minute, before Franco stopped him and translated.

"He says—and I am paraphrasing his speech—that he was my age when the American came with the letter. Paulo did not want the responsibility of holding it so long. Nor did his partner. But the man insisted. With tears in his eyes, he begged them to take it, to keep it safe. So they accepted his letter and put it away. It has been here ever since. New park rangers have asked about it so many times over the years that a type of legend grew up around it. Some made bets whether anyone would ever come to claim it, or if it would remain here until the Day of Judgment."

"Well, I'm here now," I said. "Thank you for keeping it safe all these years."

I turned and, letter in hand, left the guard shack. Outside, I ambled absentmindedly over to a trickling stream that cut through the campground. My fingers worked beneath the brittle, aged glue sealing the envelope shut. Just as I was about to remove and read the paper inside, a voice stopped me.

"You should wait," Franco said, materializing at my side.

Quizzically, perhaps with a pinch of irritation, I asked him why.

"Because you are not at the Torres, and the envelope instructs that you should read the letter there."

I turned it over to read the front again. "Isn't that where we are?" I asked. "Isn't this the Torres campground?"

Franco chuckled. His brown eyes were warm with amusement as he replied, "Yes, that is its name, because this is the closest campground *before* the Torres. The three sharp spires at the top of this mountain—*these* are the Torres. If you keep following the path a few kilometers past this campground, you will arrive at a lake. The Torres themselves are on the other side of the lake, but that is where the people observe them."

"OK!" I replied. "Thanks for the tip! I'll head up there now."

Really I just wanted to read your letter at the campground so I could move on to the next leg of this trip, but I suppose I should play by your rules. You *did* invent the game, after all.

Again, Franco stopped me. "Not tonight," he said. "It is too late in the evening and would be nearly dark by the time you arrived. You have a large backpack. I assume it is filled with camping gear. Stay here for the night. In the morning I will guide you up the path to the lake. There is a special place at the top where tourists are not supposed to go, but nowhere is off-limits for a ranger. From here, you will have the most beautiful and solitary view of the Torres. It will be perfect for reading your letter."

That streamside conversation with Franco actually took place hours ago. Since then, he has gone above and beyond for me. I must look pretty helpless to a seasoned outdoorsman like himself. When he found out I had never set up a tent before, had never even *camped* before, he took the next hour off in order to assist me. Pole by pole, he showed me how to construct your two-person tent. He also pointed out that I could cram a bunch of clothes in the sleeping bag's cover sack and turn it into a pillow, because I didn't bring one along. Since my water supply was running low, he taught me how to use your handpump water filter so that I can draw drinkable water up from the stream.

As Franco did all this, I imagined you doing the same sorts of things. How many times did your hands erect this tent? Did you ever use that pillow trick, stuffing your clothes into your sleeping bag sack? How many gallons of water did the strength of your arms pump through that filter?

Somewhere along the pathway of my musings, I realized something.

I never knew you. Not really. Some former version of me did, but not my current, conscious self. Now I'm using all this gear from your life, envisioning you lying here in this very tent so long ago, and I have to say ... I miss you. And I miss everything *you* were supposed to teach me but never could. It was nice of Franco to help out today, but it should have been *you,* Dad.

Aaaaand there's that whiny, cheated feeling again. I've avoided it for twenty years, but suddenly I can't seem to shake it anymore. You're finally haunting me. I hope you're at least a friendly ghost.

So here I am, sitting next to a tiny fire, hungry because I thought (like an idiot) that a couple Clif bars would be enough food after a six-mile hike, using your headlamp to write in one of your blank journals. In a few minutes, I'll crawl into your tent, where I hope my exhausted ass can slip into nothingness for a few hours.

And all I can wonder is ... will your sleeping bag still smell like you?

Even if it does, I would never know. Somehow that makes me sadder than ever before.

Can't wait to read your letter tomorrow. (Honestly, it's taking every ounce of willpower I possess to not rip open this envelope right this very second!)

Sleep tight, Dad. If sleep is even a thing where you are.

Love, your (melancholy) little girl,
Kate

February 4th, 2003

Dear Kate—

The first time I laid eyes upon these spires called the *Torres,* I was only twenty-four years old. The icy breath of the wind sweeping down from their jagged faces and across the glacial lake below could have chilled the devil himself. My skin crawled with goosebumps, but I would have happily frozen to death right there, basking in the glory of Torres del Paine's crown jewel. It's the sort of otherworldly scene you can't fully believe exists until its image is printed directly onto your own two retinas, and afterward you are left with an indelible photograph in your mind's eye. It's the sort of memory you know you'll never forget until the day you die.

How long have they stood here, I wondered, even then, *keeping watch over this place? How many ages have come and gone, as these stone sentinels remain, unmoved and unshaken? How many eons may still pass before they crumble and fall into memory and then obscurity?*

On that crisp, February afternoon, the mighty Torres became a symbol for me. They were an icon of strength, stalwart and loyal at their post atop Patagonia's most magnificent park.

The moment you were born, Kate, I was determined to become one myself. A tower, a guardian, a source of strength and safety and infallible protection for my daughter, who had become my own heart. The time had arrived to put foolish, selfish youth behind me. You gave your dad a purpose far greater and more noble than himself.

In all my wildest nightmares, I never thought that at thirty-three years old, this brand-new father would find out he was dying. Both my parents had passed away young, one in an accident and the other from cancer. It always felt like a given that I would outlive them.

Then came the diagnosis. It's strange to hear such an earthshaking statement from a doctor. It comes across almost like a decree: "Thou shalt not live beyond two more years." When you're as young as I was, it sounds more like a tasteless joke than anything.

But the nightmare was sadly, terribly, real.

Please know that I fought it. First, I fought the diagnosis itself. I sought second and third opinions from different doctors. When they didn't give me what I was looking for, I turned the fight toward finding a treatment, *something* that would cure me—or at the very least give me more time. I tried to fight with diet and exercise, with meditation and yoga and whatever other crap I thought might add even a couple days to my life. I became blinded, lost in my quest to survive.

Oddly enough, it was your mother, who loves me more than anything, that finally convinced me to stop. She helped me realize that in fighting for more time, I was actually squandering the precious days I had remaining.

That's when I started pouring the last of myself into you and your mom. It's when I came up with the idea for these letters, my final gift to you.

A final gift of strength for my baby girl.

But I do think you should hear the reason why I fought so damn hard at first. It was all for *you.* If I'm being honest, your mom was a much smaller motivation. She had made a choice to accept what was happening. She was *able* to make that choice. Our years, though short, have been beautiful, and she's a strong enough person to walk away with joy and thankfulness for what we shared.

You, however, were too young to make that kind of decision for yourself. That never seemed fair in my eyes. One day, when old enough, you would realize that everyone else had a dad except you. You would discover a hole in your life that you could never refill. I don't know why, but that realization bothered me more than anything else. I wanted to be there for you—yes, for my selfish reasons, so I could have the joy of watching you grow, but also because it pained me worse than my sickness to know that you would live without the protecting arms of a father in your life.

Even as I write this now, I can't completely quiet that voice. The unsettling, unceasing whisper telling me I've failed you. That's a gnawing thought to live with.

And to die with.

So you will have to find the strength elsewhere. Undoubtedly you'll have much in yourself, but the truth is that none of us is meant to stand on our own. Human beings, even when we don't want to admit it, always draw on the power and courage and protection of others. For as much as our culture glorifies independence, we are utterly, hopelessly reliant creatures.

I don't know who the other towers in your life will be. Certainly your mom will lend as much of her strength as she can give. Perhaps you will find a guardian fortress also in a stepfather—though I'm about as welcoming of that notion as I am of having my nose glued to my butt—or in your grandparents, or in one of your uncles or aunts, or an inspiring teacher, or a husband, or even one of your own children! Whenever and however that strength is offered to you someday, promise me this: that you will welcome it and treasure it, and that you will give your own strength in return.

This is how we are meant to stand. This is how we are meant to live. I have given you as much of myself as I could. I can still give a little more. But my soul will leave this earth comforted, knowing that even as my "tower" crumbles and falls, there will be many more to stand with you. To strengthen you. To protect you.

To keep watch over my life's greatest treasure.

I love you now and always,
Dad

The next phase of your journey is some well-deserved rest! If you managed to keep pace, I have to imagine a new college semester will be starting soon. Obviously my little scavenger hunt is the most important thing you've ever done, but that doesn't mean you can't also make time for other important things!

As for the next letter location, I'll be sending you to America's "last great frontier": Alaska. From Anchorage, you'll have to travel north to Denali National Park, the home of Mt. McKinley, our continent's highest peak. Once there, acquire the proper permits and ride the bus to the Eielson Visitor Center, where you'll hop off and take a multi-day backpacking trip up to Anderson Pass. Scour the saddle between the mountains there until you find a circle of black rocks. Directly beneath its center is where you'll find my next letter. Beware, you'll have to dig a bit, so bring either a dog or a shovel with you!

Enjoy your time off until the summer thaw. Best of luck when you finally do embark on your next journey. Be smart and be safe. After all, you are *headed to grizzly country!*

January 8, 2023

Dear Dad,

How can you be so flowery, so eloquent, *and* so stupid all at once?

Here I sit, right where you sat all those years ago. Here I stare up at the same trio of razor-thin peaks, rising at the far side of this milky sapphire lake as if grown from its waters. Here I pull my jacket—your windbreaker—snug against my body to shut out the same bitter breeze. Here I have just finished reading your letter, which even now is pressed safely inside the back cover of my journal.

Sure, you aren't alive anymore. But that certainly doesn't mean you aren't a tower of strength for your little girl. What a stupid, *stupid* thing for you to suggest! Seriously, Dad, over the past week I've learned more about myself than I have in the last decade. I've also discovered more about who I want to be than what anyone else has taught me. And guess what! You're accomplishing that from beyond the grave! Just imagine what you could pull off if you were still alive!

If that isn't evidence enough of your strength and influence in my life, I don't know what else could be. You aren't some "has-been" tower that cracked and collapsed when I was a baby. You're exactly what you set out to be the day I was born. You're my guardian. You're my protector. Even now.

But enough about you. Let's talk about me.

My morning began balls-early when Franco arrived at my tent with some kind of energy bar and a cup of the nastiest, shit-for-beans coffee I've ever tasted. Still, it was a toasty drink on a frosty morning and desperately needed. I pinched my nose and gulped it down.

Instead of taking offense at my grumpy, daybreak rudeness, he chuckled and said, "They do not exactly stock our guard huts with Starbucks. It's instant coffee, but it does what it is supposed to do."

"Yeah. Thanks," I replied, handing him the empty mug.

"Put on some warmer clothes," he ordered, speaking as if I had no choice, "and meet me at the guardhouse when you are ready. We have a bit of a climb, and you want to beat the other tourists to the top."

What I wanted more than anything was to curl up in the warmth of my sleeping bag and catch a couple more hours of shuteye. Somehow, I managed to coax my stiff muscles into my hiking clothes and convince myself that another two miles after yesterday's six would be no big deal.

On our way to the top, Franco distracted me from the cold and my aching body by asking everything he could about my life. For someone whose native tongue is Spanish, he's remarkably fluent speaking English. I told him all about life in Denver, described Mom, shared a few stories of stupid high school escapades involving Emma and my other friends, and explained what I was studying in my junior year at the University of Wyoming. I talked about waitressing at Chili's and all my favorite Denver sports teams. The one topic I couldn't seem to bring up was Andrew, not even when he asked if there was a significant other waiting for me back home. I merely gave a nervous chuckle and turned the questioning around by asking about *his* life.

Franco, it turns out, is six years older than me. He was born and raised in a city called Arica, which is apparently about as far north as Chile grows people. He spent his final year of high school in the United States as an exchange student (which is apparently why he speaks such fluent

English). When Franco was in his teens, he and his family vacationed here in Torres del Paine. Years later, Franco says he came to a crossroads in life. That's when he remembered these mountains and returned permanently to become a ranger.

"So this is home?" I asked him, thinking back to my conversation with Bret and Jezzi at the hostel. It's still a foreign notion for me to think of *home* as transcending the suburban, brick-and-mortar terms I'm so accustomed to.

Franco grinned sideways and shot me a "screw-you-for-asking-a-question-that-deep" look. For a moment he stayed silent, and I knew I'd crossed some undefined line. Then he said, "I don't know where home is. It isn't Arica any longer. Of that I am sure. But here?" He shrugged, then stared at the trail ahead and said no more.

We stayed silent until the summit. When the trail crested the slope and opened onto a handful of tourists leaning over their tripod-mounted cameras, I knew we had reached the top. Spread out before me were the tranquil lake and its guardian towers, thrust toward the heavens like the spearheads of giants.

"Come this way," Franco beckoned. He led me over a gravel path and away from the other vista viewers. As if he owned the whole mountain, he walked straight past a sign that read *PROHIBITO EL PASO.* I don't remember much of my high school Spanish, but I've retained enough to know that it translates to *NO TRESPASSING* in English. After another five silent minutes clambering across steep scree and small boulders, Franco faced the jagged, triple spires of the Torres and raised his arms.

"Here they are!" He made the declaration as if he were introducing the headliner at a rock concert. Then, much more gently: "And here you may open your letter."

I was sure he'd sit next to me and try to read over my shoulder. Hell, it's exactly what I would have done in his situation. After the years of mystery and intrigue, who could blame him? Instead, Franco winked a kind, chocolatey brown eye at me and sauntered away.

I sat, alone. I read. I cried a little.

When I was finished reading and had put your letter back into the envelope, Franco returned and knelt beside me. He must have been watching from nearby. I could see the questions raging inside him, yet he neither said nor asked anything. With his fingers laced together, he gazed up at the monolithic towers, which were now painted blaze orange by the rising sun.

Unable to stand his casual nonchalance, I waved the envelope in front of his face and asked, "Well? Don't you want to know what it says?" After all, he and every other Torres ranger for the last fifth of a century have been waiting for an answer to that very question.

Franco never broke his gaze away from the spires as he said, "No. Some things are meant to stay between a father and his daughter."

"How'd you know that's what this was?" I inquired, suddenly on the warpath. I hadn't mentioned anything about the letter's author being my dad. "Did you read it?"

"Of course not," Franco replied coolly. "But only a dying father would do something like this for his little girl."

Damn. He is one astute sonofabitch.

Franco stood and ambled down the slope toward the congregating tourists. I can't be sure, but I thought I noticed something of a sadness in his face as he turned from me. Looks like I found me an old softie out here in the Chilean mountains! I can only wonder what that sudden shadow over his otherwise sunny demeanor was all about ...

I suppose it's time to put this journal away again. I'll sit a moment longer, letting the power and majesty of this image ink a permanent photograph into the scrapbook of my mind. I'll take a picture with your camera too. And then I'll say goodbye to Franco and begin my long migration home.

As I do, I will thank God again, and again, and again that I have a watch-tower like you standing guard over my life. Looking out for me. Protecting me. Loving me. And, in your own way, raising me.

Love, your (treasured) little girl,
Kate

January 8, 2023 … again

Dear Dad,

Highly irregular, I know, but after my hike back to the guardhouse with Franco, I felt like a second entry for January 8 was in order.

After leaving the Torres, we trudged a half-mile down the trail in a long and awkward silence. The tension of my accusation hung in the air. I had only met Franco yesterday but strangely felt like I'd just betrayed my best friend. Why did I have to suggest that he had read your letter? Apologies and I have never been close friends, so even though I knew I was in the wrong, the word *sorry* just wasn't escaping my stubborn lips.

Apparently Franco's tension was of a different source than my own, because he suddenly blurted out, "This isn't home."

"What?" I asked, caught off guard and a bit confused. "What about home?"

"You asked earlier if this place was home for me," he clarified. "It is not."

"Then … where is home?" I asked.

Franco shrugged, kicked at a pebble, and answered, "I don't know. When I first came here, I thought this was home. But after a while, I realized I was mistaken."

He must have noticed my look of surprise, the one wordlessly saying *I can't believe anyone could be discontent in a place as beautiful as this,* because he went on. "Please, do not misunderstand me. A part of my soul will always belong here. I do love this place. But there is so much more to the world, to *life,* than to spend my years rotating from ranger post to ranger post. There are always people around me, yet it is a lonely existence."

I didn't say anything, mostly because I was totally unsure *what* to say. Here this man, little more than a stranger, was baring his heart to me.

Maybe it's just me who sucks at feelings? Then again ...

"I don't know where home is either." The words burst through my lips before I realized I was saying them. Once I'd started, it didn't seem right to stop, so I continued. "I mean, I have a mom who loves me. She's taken care of me my whole life, and we're really close. And I have aunts and uncles and a grandpa, and they basically all adore me. And that might be a *comfortable* place for me, but is it really *home?* Is it where I feel settled and at peace and fulfilled? I don't know. I don't think so."

Franco nodded politely at a trio of passing tourists, then asked, "Where do you think home is?"

"Not sure. But I think maybe you don't know for sure ... until you know for sure."

Franco laughed (I've noticed he likes to laugh) and replied, "Well said. Clear as dirty dishwater."

I rolled my eyes. "Whatever. I can't think of a better way to put it."

After mulling a moment over what I'd so poorly stated, he spoke up again. "I understand what you mean. Maybe you are correct. But it also makes me afraid. It sounds like that could be a terrible, long journey, and one with no certainty of ever finding my—or your—real home."

"True," I muttered, "but maybe that's part of the reason why my dad sent me on this weird scavenger hunt. To help me figure out the answers to some of these tough questions."

"What is that? 'Scavenger hunt'?" Franco asked, his English failing him for the first time since we'd started talking.

"It's a sort of game, I guess. It's like when someone gives you clues to go and find something. Or maybe a bunch of different things that you collect and bring back with you."

He let this sink in for a moment. Then, with lucid realization, he said, "So the Torres were not your first stop."

"No. This was my third. My dad also sent me to my grandpa's house and Norway."

"Norway!" Franco whistled through his teeth. "You are lucky, Kate Jackson."

I glanced sideways at him and, stupidly, replied, "Yeah?"

"Lucky to have a father who loved you enough to show you the world," he explained. His dark chocolate eyes had become drills now boring into my own. He held my gaze for a single second, but it felt like minutes. Then he said, "I envy you."

Like earlier, I vomited my next words before my brain had the chance to stifle them. "Maybe you could come with me."

Franco stopped. His mouth opened and closed wordlessly, like a fish out of water gasping for air, before he finally said, "It is your journey."

Since there was no taking back what I had said, I decided to double down.

"Yeah. That's true. But that doesn't mean it can't also be *your* journey. Plus, I have a sneaking suspicion this little scavenger hunt is only gonna get harder. I could probably use some backup."

Things quieted down for the next stretch of our descent. I could see his brain spinning like a truck tire in a muddy rut. What I had said caught him off guard, throwing off the balance of the life he's cultivated for himself the past few years.

Franco's silence broke when we sat to rest on a large boulder. He asked, "Where is your father sending you next?"

"Denali National Park. In Alaska. It sounds like it'll be a legit backpacking trip through the wilderness. Not like anything I've done before."

"Alaska," he mused after a sip from his canteen. He sounded almost nostalgic. "I have often dreamed of seeing the grizzly bears there. They were my favorite animal when I was a child."

"I mean, obviously I won't be going for a while," I said, ignoring his grizzly bear lust. "It's the middle of winter right now. But this summer, when the snow melts, you could meet me there."

He laughed lightly and replied, "Then it seems I have some time before you need an answer. I will think it over. Your offer is ... very tempting, I admit."

The rest of the hike was spent enjoying comfortable small talk. He told me about some of the park's other exquisite locations and its abundant wildlife. He explained to me that the llama-looking creatures I saw on my hike up the mountain are, in fact, relatives of llamas called *guanacos.* He also pointed out an Andean condor soaring high overhead and shared the story of the bird's struggle against extinction.

All in all, it was a wonderful morning. One of the best I've ever had.

I felt an odd pang of loss when I said goodbye to someone I've only known for half a day. After packing my tent and belongings, I gave him a slip of paper with my email address and phone number. He hugged me, and I hugged him back. Then I turned and walked away from him and out of his life, probably forever.

As I descended back through the subalpine forest and along the river-cut clove between the mountains, I questioned why I had done what I did. Why did I invite a mere acquaintance to join me on this intimate journey of rediscovering my dead dad?

By the end of the trail, I determined I'd done it to get back at Andrew. Our last conversation was so angry, so sharp with disagreement. His tone was condescending and possessive. It was like he owned me and thus had rights to me. I know I decided to treat him with a little more patience and understanding, but it sure seemed to me like he was crossing a line.

Maybe he just misses me. Maybe he's worried, and this is how he handles worry. Either way, it's no excuse. I guess we'll have some things to sort through when I get home.

Anyway, I'm currently on the bus back to Puerto Natales. I guess it's time now for some rest and a break and then more school. I can already foresee a young woman sitting at her desk with a *very* distracted mind, as I wonder what Alaska has in store for me. Six months is a long wait ... but I guess I don't have much choice! It'll at least give me lots of time to plan.

Don't worry, though. I'm sure I'll concoct a few reasons to write you between now and then!

Love, your (impatient) little girl,
Kate

---------- FOUR ----------

The Long Pause

January 11, 2023

Dear Dad,

I don't know if I've ever felt so damn miserable in my entire life.

I was expecting Mom at the airport this afternoon. Instead it was Andrew waiting for me beyond the security gate. He was holding up a cheesy sign with my name on it. I tensed immediately, my stomach suddenly made of more knots than you'd find on a sailboat. Besides the fact that I had neither showered, nor brushed my teeth, nor slept much in the past day and a half, we also hadn't spoken a word since our Norway blowout.

He wrapped me in a tight hug. His stubbled chin rested on my forehead as he said, "I'm so happy to see you, Kate. I know you were expecting your mom, but I talked her into letting me come instead."

"It's good to see you too," I replied heavily. The half-hearted words seemed to stick on my fuzzy, unbrushed tongue.

Andrew gave me a quick kiss. Instantly, he regretted it. His face screwed up with disgust as he snickered and said, "No toothpaste where you came from?"

"No showers, either," I said, noticing in the light, back-and-forth banter an immediate easing of my apprehension.

"Or beds, I'm guessing. No offense, but you look a little like something from *The Walking Dead.*"

"It's a little hard not to take offense at that, but 36 hours of airplanes and airports'll do that to a gal," I said. I pulled him into another hug, this time with about 80% heart. In moments, our old, carefree, pre-New Year's relationship had returned. The one we had *before* all that talk about the future.

"Extra big tip if you can get me home and into a shower in less than thirty," I told him, pulling away from his arms again. "Or 45, I guess. Forgot I had to check my bag."

The gods must have known I needed a miracle, because my bright blue backpack was the first item to slide onto the luggage carousel. Andrew grabbed it for me. I stumbled at his side to the parking garage and his car like I'd been bitten by a narcoleptic zombie.

The next thing I knew, we were parked in the driveway at home. Andrew had already turned off the Mazda and opened my door by the time I awoke.

"I know how much you hate it when people overuse the word *literally*, but I literally don't think I've ever seen anyone fall asleep faster than that," he said, taking my hand and helping me out of the car. "You didn't even have time to put on your seatbelt!"

Mom was waiting inside with a million questions. By the time I'd answered the first couple, however, she could tell I was in no state for an interview.

"Why don't you go upstairs, Little Love," she suggested. "Take a shower and a nap. Andrew and I can hang out for a while before you head out to dinner."

"Dinner?" I repeated.

"Sorry," Andrew apologized. "You fell asleep so fast I didn't have time to tell you, but I got us a reservation at Churrasco de Brasilia tonight. Sort of a 'welcome home' thing."

"That's super sweet of you," I told him, sensing some of that tension return, "but honestly, I'm so frickin' tired. I want to sleep until, like, February."

Andrew's grin faltered. He shoved his hands into his pockets and toed distractedly at the carpet. A desperation-tinted note of demand overtook his voice as he said, "Well, the reservation isn't until eight. Can't you take a break from sleeping to have dinner with me for an hour?"

"I'm just so exhausted."

"Come on, please?" he goaded. Moving on to the guilt trip, he added, "I haven't seen you in two weeks."

I simply didn't have the energy to argue, so I said, "Wake me up at 7:15, and we'll see how I'm feeling."

He must have understood from my tone that I was done with the conversation. He nodded his agreement, and I dragged my exhausted ass upstairs. One steaming shower later, I was buried a mile beneath my covers and fast asleep.

As my vision transitioned from dream world to waking one, it was Mom's face I saw hovering over mine. Her hand was resting gently on my shoulder as I came to and pushed myself into a seated position against the headboard. She brushed my blond hair away from my eyes and tucked it behind my ear, just like she'd done a billion times during my childhood.

"Hey there, Little Love," she whispered with a wink. She's used that nickname for as long as I can remember. It's something of a joke between us now because of how hard I rebelled against it in middle school.

"Andrew still here?" I asked, praying for *no* but sickly certain of *yes.*

Mom nodded. In her staring sapphire eyes I read exactly what she didn't need to say.

"I know, I know," I mumbled annoyedly. "I have to go with him."

"Look," she said, tapping my chest just above my heart, "I don't know what's going on in here, but I do know that boy's been dying for you to come home. Most days he texted me to ask if I'd heard anything from you. He cares about you a lot, Kate. The least you can give back to someone who cares that much is a couple hours at dinner."

I simultaneously rolled my eyes and chuckled, then said, "Whatever. You're right. You're always right. So annoying. I guess sleep can wait."

"Yes, it can," she agreed. "And it'll also have to wait when you get back home, because other than two pathetically short messages, I haven't heard a thing about your trip!" She waggled a finger in front of my disheveled head and added, "But right now, you need to do something about this mess."

She left, and I gave myself the NASCAR pit stop of personal spruce-ups, wrangling my tangled hair into a ponytail and painting a coat of makeup on myself in about 45 seconds. I hurriedly wrestled myself into a sweater and hoisted a pair of jeans up around my waist. I was aware my appearance wasn't exactly fitting for a date at a fancy Brazilian steakhouse, but compared to the past week, I was dressed like Kate freaking Middleton.

Andrew was reading something on his phone when I tromped down the stairs. He glanced up, whistled, and said, "You clean up nice." Behind his beaming face, though, I sensed uneasiness, distraction, like someone trying their hardest to smile during a funeral.

"Ready?" I asked, relieved to discover that he was also wearing jeans. A red-and-white-checkered, button-down shirt and charcoal-gray windbreaker completed his ensemble.

Keeping his hands shoved into his coat pockets, Andrew led the way to his steel-blue hatchback. He opened the door for me, a gesture I'd always found genuine and sweet, then jumped in himself and sped us toward the restaurant. We didn't say much as we drove. A tension, palpable enough to raise the hair on my neck, had returned. I knew he felt it too.

"So?" he finally asked. "Want to tell me about South America? Chile?"

"It was ... beautiful," I said. "So was my dad's letter."

"Where you off to next?" he retorted, firing off the question a little too rapidly, as if the bullet had been preloaded into the chamber. It sounded more like an accusation than a genuine question.

"Nowhere," I replied with an airy sigh. "Not yet, at least. He's sending me to Alaska, but that one will have to wait until summer."

Andrew's shoulders relaxed immediately. "Good," he said.

"Good?" I echoed. The edge in Andrew's voice must have been a super contagion, because I was suddenly infected also.

"Sorry," he muttered, attempting to backpedal quicker than a cyclist spotting a cliff. "It's just ... you know ... I've missed you."

"It was only two weeks!" I exclaimed through clenched teeth, unable to keep my rising temper from raising my volume.

"I—yes—you're right," he stammered. The whites of his knuckles clenched around the steering wheel told me he wanted to argue, to rage, to tell me off. But something deeper, perhaps his overwhelming desire to hang on to me, was suppressing him. "In the grand scheme of things, I guess two weeks isn't much."

And there it was. Just like that, we were right back to Christmas. In his mind he had already cemented us as a couple, not only now but indefinitely.

Suddenly, it all clicked. Why he'd come to pick me up at the airport. Why he'd been so adamant we go out for dinner. Why he'd kept his hands shoved in his pockets.

He was making sure his valuable secret didn't slip out. There was a ring in there.

Andrew was planning to propose. My former nightmares about his secret "plan" for New Year's Eve were now becoming reality, albeit a week late.

I said nothing, just stared over at him. I wanted to soak him in one more time, to assess him and see him as if this were one of our first dates. Handsome? Absolutely. The dusty, wavy hair, the sea-green eyes, the basketball player's frame—it all makes him a magnet for many an undergraduate girl's gaze. Perhaps even a few professors let their eyes drift when he leaves their classrooms. And his personality? Nobody's perfect, of course, but he's charming, able to hold an engaging conversation, witty, hardworking, and generally kind.

But now everything was turning cloudy. I wanted so badly to see what I used to see, for my heart to flutter over his warm eyes the way it once did. A piece of that affection was still there, lingering, but a shadow had eclipsed the rest. To Andrew our future was set in stone, but to me everything was quicksand.

I knew what I had to do. The realization was like swallowing a shot of month-old milk. Instantly, I felt sick.

Yet it had to be done.

"Andrew, we need to take a break."

I won't dig into the rest of the details, Dad, but I've never voluntarily done anything that's made me so miserable. It's damn difficult to watch a grown man sob through your own glassy tears as you apologize over and over for what you know is the right thing to do.

Only when he had finally resigned himself to my decision did he turn the car around. We spoke little after that. He dropped me off at the end of my driveway. I held him one more time with all my strength, truly not wanting to let him go.

But then I did, and Andrew drove away.

I know I won't be able to avoid him for long once the new semester starts. The Wyoming campus isn't very big. Sooner or later we'll run into each other, and we'll have to reexamine our relationship. I hope I have my head straight and my heart back in order when that happens. Andrew isn't the kind of guy who will wait around forever.

Nor should he.

I guess time will tell the rest of our story. I'll just have to be patient and wait.

As for my present role in the story, it continued that night with Mom. When I walked in the door less than 45 minutes after leaving, she realized something was wrong. By now she knows how I feel about feelings, so instead of asking me what happened with Andrew, she said, "Well? Are you ready to tell me about your dad's crazy trip?"

Three hours (and a couple glasses of wine) later, here I am. No boyfriend. No school or work for the next week. Nowhere to go. Just me and my dumbass, overactive brain, thinking over and over and over about everything that happened tonight.

Maybe you didn't have the ability to see the future after all. If you could, I want you to know you're a real dick for not giving me a distraction. You could have sent me *somewhere.* Like to the Moon or Mars or maybe the sun. Anywhere would be better than my current circle of hell.

If you do have any ideas, send me a sign ASAP.

Love, your (drained) little girl,
Kate

January 30, 2023

Dear Dad,

I had more or less given up on ever hearing from Franco again. After all, I gave him my contact information but didn't receive any in return, and you can't exactly look up *Torres Guard Shack* in the white pages. Then, out of the blue, he emailed me today and said he's been considering my offer. A few weeks of deliberation apparently convinced him to take the plunge and join me in Alaska this summer! It'll be nice to see him again. This may sound stupid, but during our short time together, I felt like I was walking and talking with a kindred soul. Maybe Franco is my spirit animal.

So that's one thing I've got going on. The other is that I saw Andrew yesterday. It was the first time since I hit *PAUSE* on our relationship. Like I already said, it was inevitable. Campus isn't large enough to hide me forever. We didn't speak or anything. I just caught a glimpse of him from a distance. I know this might come across weird, or maybe even hypocritical, but my heart rebroke a little. It almost feels like my best friend died three weeks ago, and I'm the one who killed him. I confided so much of myself to him, and now he's gone. Free. Cut loose. Technically, I guess I told him we needed to "take a break," but for some reason it feels so much more permanent than that.

It had to be done. For both our sakes. I know that, and no part of me doubts I did the right thing.

Doesn't make it any easier.

I put together a box of his things a couple days ago. You know, the kinds of random knickknacks you borrow and share and mingle together over the months: movies, sweatshirts, books, coffee mugs. Soon I hope I'm a little less of a damn coward. Then I may actually work up the courage to call him and arrange an exchange. Lord knows he's got plenty of my stuff too! Part of me wants to think meeting up could pave a road to reconciliation. Deep down, though, I know that isn't going to happen. I know that *shouldn't* happen.

Anyway, I just wanted to give you an update about these goings-on. I have no idea how much longer this journal needs to last (since the extent of your scavenger hunt remains a complete mystery to me), so I guess I better cut this short before I start wasting too much paper. I'm sure I'll still check in once or twice before Alaska, but those entries may be few and far between. It's not as though I don't care about you, of course. But if these pages *are* our connection somehow—our Bivrost—I don't want to squander them on the mundane details of college life.

Love, your (patiently-waiting-for-more) little girl,
Kate

February 7, 2023

Dear Dad,

Today was the day. I finally screwed up the courage to arrange the exchange with Andrew. He came by my dorm with a box of my things, where I was waiting with a box of his. We chitchatted for a couple minutes about nothing, and he went on his way. I guess I expected more drama, maybe even a bit of a fight from him, but he seemed resigned to the fact, if not a touch defeated. It could be that, after the dust settled, he also realized something about our relationship was off.

There was that lingering part of me that wanted to admit I was wrong, a voice inside screaming that we should get back together. I'm not sure, though, if that voice is the real me. I think it's the insecure part of myself, that corner of my soul which knows Andrew means a comfortable future. But there is an even more powerful beast inside me, and she is the one calling the shots now. She knows Andrew is safe, but she also knows that doesn't necessarily make him *right.*

Whatever the case, it means I have my *Mean Girls* DVD back, along with a couple coffee mugs and the copy of my favorite book, *East of Eden,* which I stole from your old bookshelf. Looks like my Friday night activities are set! (Does that make me a loser?) Other than a few odds and ends, there was nothing else valuable or important inside the box. Makes me wonder why I wanted my stuff back so badly. On a subconscious level, maybe I simply wanted to talk with Andrew one more time.

God, I'm confused. When I read what I've written so far, I kinda hate myself a little. Oh well. Onward and upward from here! I'm counting down every day until Alaska.

Love, your (*im*patiently-waiting-for-more) little girl,
Kate

March 31, 2023

Dear Dad,

I miss writing to you. I'm trying to conserve the blank pages of this journal, but in doing so I have the daily sense that something important keeps slipping past me. I could buy myself another journal and write more, but the very idea of it feels wrong, like I'm cheating on the one you gave me.

Today, however, was important enough to send you a quick note, because I finally bought my ticket to Anchorage! I'm leaving June 18, which should put me in Denali for the solstice. I've read so much about the midnight sun and the eternal day of summer. Seeing it for myself will be an experience to remember my whole life, I'm sure.

In other news, Franco and I have been emailing regularly over the past month. We've even video-chatted three times now. Turns out he's rather handy when it comes to planning these types of serious backpacking trips! His current plan is to meet me in Anchorage. He's renting a car at the airport there, and together we'll drive to the park. Once he's helped me find your letter, I'll move on to the next leg of the scavenger hunt while he stays in Alaska. He decided to extend his trip so he can camp and backpack and sightsee longer.

Afterward, who knows? Franco has already determined that he will resign from his Torres ranger position at the beginning of summer. Apparently our mountain trail conversation was one he couldn't kick out of his mind, even after I left. He doesn't know the exact changes his life needs at this point, only that changes *are* needed. His hope is that a few distractionless weeks in Alaska will provide the clear headspace required to discover the next path he should walk.

Emma, of course, is convinced Franco is simply in love with me. According to her, I'm the sole source to blame for his confusion. She came up to Laramie last weekend to visit, which is how we found ourselves at a wine bar on Friday night. Once Veni Vidi Vino's cheapest Moscato had washed away my feelings filter, I started telling her all about Franco.

Big mistake. Emma looped her fingers through that buttonhole and refused to let go.

"Ooooooo, sounds sexy!" she exclaimed. "Also, you suck. You went to South America, got yourself a Latin lover, and didn't even tell your best friend!?"

"Whoa! Slow down, like, half a second," I said, already regretting that I'd opened my stupid mouth. "I never said this was a *love* thing."

Emma waved dismissively and replied, "Oh, please. He's obviously in love with you, Kate. He wouldn't commit to such a long and expensive trip if he only had friend feelings for you."

"We haven't spent enough time together for that," I countered, hurriedly rebuilding my defensive walls. "Sure, we get along, but that doesn't mean much. I get along with lots of people. Doesn't automatically mean *love.* Besides, I still don't know where things stand with Andrew."

She rolled her eyes and scoffed playfully. "Yes you do. It's been three months. You already traded your stuff back. If you were getting back together, you would have done it already." She leaned toward me and lowered her voice to a more serious timbre. "Trust me, Kate. It's time to move on from domestic boys. Spend some time ... *south* of the border."

I should have expected this exact reaction from her. Emma is a dive-right-in sorta person. If you weren't already able to deduce it by my many other heel-dragging episodes in this journal, I travel through life heeding its *CAUTION* signs. Better safe than sorry, right?

"Don't be gross about it, you perv," I said, kicking her lightly. I read into her "south of the border" comment exactly what she'd intended. "We'll see how it goes once I spend a few days in Alaska with him."

"That's all I ask of you," Emma replied. Then, brightening up, she added, "And if things don't work out for you, you can give him my number! I'd be more than happy to take him off your hands ... or any other parts."

Following the millionth roll of my eyes, I moved the conversation along to topics less personal. Truthfully, I'm still unsure where I stand with all this Franco business. But I am certain of one thing: You would have liked him, Dad. He has an adventurous spirit and a kind heart, just like the person writing to me in all your letters. And, if I'm being totally honest, he's pretty easy on the eyes. Emma got that right, at least!

Sorry. I know dads prefer not to hear their daughters talk about boys. But I'm beginning to think that, with Franco, I might be regaining some of the closeness and camaraderie I lost in Andrew. Obviously it's too early to know much with any degree of certainty (I've only spent a grand total of one day with the guy), but there might be some potential ...?

You don't have to worry, though. I'll make sure he keeps his hands off me when we're alone in the Alaskan wilderness. We'll probably be so busy fighting off bears and wolverines and shit, he won't have time to try any of Emma's "south of the border" funny business.

Alright. One more class and then I'm home for the weekend. Mom says she has news and wants to tell me in person ...

Love, your (nervous-that-mom-has-a-boyfriend) little girl,
Kate

April 1, 2023

Dear Dad,

I have some baaaaaaaad news to break to you. Are you sitting down? *Can* you sit down up there?

If not, just lean back against a cloud and listen.

My fears were confirmed this morning when Mom took me out for brunch at Pete's Diner. Turns out our table for two was actually set for three.

Mom was as cute as a dewdrop on a baby bunny's nose the whole time. I could tell she was nervous for me to meet her new suitor, which I knew meant she must like him an awful lot. She fidgeted back and forth in her chair, sharing interesting facts about him and his kids and his career, trying to stimulate conversation between me and him by pointing out mutual interests.

Once brunch was finished and we'd stuffed ourselves silly with waffles and pancakes and biscuits with sausage gravy, Mom and I got in the car to head home. No sooner had we left the strip mall's parking lot than she calmly asked what I thought about him.

Maybe before I share my review with you, Dad, I should tell you a little about him.

His name is Gary Gorszozski. He's a couple years older than Mom. I'm guessing Polish. He has salt-and-pepper hair, dark blue eyes, a scruffy beard ...

AND I HATE HIM SO SO MUCH! *WHY IS MOM RUINING MY LIFE?!!?*

At least that's what I'm supposed to say, right? When Mom gets herself a shiny new boyfriend, and he isn't my dad? Like, *how* could she betray you, her one and only true love, as if you meant nothing at all?

I promise, that's how I *wanted* to feel when I met him. I desired nothing more than to hate his stupid guts and declare that he'd never be good enough for Mom because he'd never be as good as you.

But dammit if I didn't like the guy ... Oops! Maybe my soft spot comes from the fact that he's a widower who lost his wife to cancer six years ago. He also happens to work in the Broncos' marketing department and can get us into games for free, so that little perk might have played a teeny tiny role in my affinity for him.

Either way, I walked away from the brunch completely emptied of my misgivings. He seems like he has his life put together, and I can see in his smiling eyes how much he cares about Mom. Plus, he has a pair of daughters who are two and four years older than me, so if things work out, it means I finally get the sisters I asked Santa for when I was little!

Sorry if you're taking all this as a betrayal. You can disown me, disinherit me if you want ...

But I haven't witnessed that glow on Mom's face for as far back as I can remember. The only time I've ever seen it is when I look at pictures of her with you. So as far as I'm concerned, that glow counts for an awful lot.

She's given you a proper mourning period, Dad. Twenty years is a good, long while to hold on to someone. And even though I know she'll never fully let you go, she deserves a *living* companion with whom she can share her life and heart. And her delicious food.

So I guess you'll have to deal with it, Dad! Besides, you have all eternity to get over her, so I'm sure you'll be cool with it sooner or later, right?

Because if not, you'll be upset for a long, looooooong time.

Love, your (treasonous) little girl,
Judas Brutus Benedict Arnold Iscariot

May 5, 2023

Dear Dad,

If the "Book of Andrew" was still an unfinished chapter in my life, this morning it was shut for good. I was hurrying across campus between classes, not paying much attention to my surroundings. At the exact moment I was about to enter Ross Hall, who comes bursting through the door? None other than Andrew himself, in the flesh.

He wasn't alone. Giggling and latched onto his upper arm was University of Wyoming's swimming superstar, national championship runner-up, Angela Martinez. She's probably a good two inches shorter than me, but in her lean, muscular, golden-curled shadow, I felt like a toddler staring up at a teacher.

Andrew was caught off guard, too. He choked out his words before I could beat him with my own. Jerk.

"Kate! Hi!" he exclaimed, a little too enthusiastic to be genuine. "I ... haven't seen you for a while. How's it going?"

My reply was interrupted before it began, as Little Miss Not-Quite-Good-Enough-For-Gold waved and announced, quite cheerily and with all the confidence of a car salesman, "I'm Ange! I don't think I've met you before."

It took every nanoparticle of my willpower not to go for the throat. Plastering on my sharkiest grin, I replied, "I'm Kate. We actually took Intro to Meteorology together freshman year." I couldn't stop myself from adding, "Andrew and I dated for a while, actually."

An expression of irritation, mixed with a dollop of fear, painted itself across Andrew's face. He chuckled nervously and said, "Yeah, for a little while. Nothing serious, though."

The feral, jealous Hyde within me, whose residual affections for Andrew had frequently beckoned me in the direction of bad decisions the last four months, almost did it. I almost called him out for the ring that had sat unused in his coat pocket that January night. I almost gloated to this sexy swimming sensation that he would be engaged to me if I hadn't broken his heart.

But I had no right, and I knew it. So instead, I simply said, "I wish I could stay and catch up, but I've gotta be at class in, like, twenty seconds."

And with that unceremonious dismissal, I swept past them and into the building.

I didn't go to class. Want to know what I did, Dad? I found a bathroom and cried. As if *I* were the one who'd gotten dumped. As if *I* were the one about to pop the question that night, only to have *him* ice our relationship.

The heart is a complicated muscle, I guess. Even if given the choice now, I don't think I'd go back to him, yet my chest hurt like a stabbing victim when I saw him with someone else. If I'm being honest, it still hurts now.

And so, once I'm finished writing this to you, I've decided I'm moving on. For good. I don't know where I'm headed (other than Alaska), but the Andrew baggage is staying behind. In a few days, I'll leave this campus. Maybe for good. Andrew will graduate and matriculate into the working world.

And it'll be like our paths never even crossed at all.

It's time for the old chapter to end and for my new chapter to begin. Where it takes me, I don't know. But I'm excited to find out.

And, Dada, despite my present sadness, I'm absolutely positively certain about one thing: The best is yet to come.

Love, your (determined) little girl,
Kate

June 17, 2023

Dear Dad,

Alright. Finally back to the main thing. T-minus 1100 hours until my blastoff from Denver International to whatever the hell the Anchorage airport is called. My bag is more packed and I'm more ready to go than John Denver himself! (Although I hope my plane fares better than the last one he boarded ... Too soon?)

I can't remember the last time I would describe myself as *giddy* with excitement, but that's exactly where my anticipation of continuing your scavenger hunt has reduced me. It feels like I had to wait a million months for this. During that time, both night and day, my obsession with your trip has swallowed up all my free time. I'm pretty sure my brain has downloaded an entire volume of Google search information, that's how much I've read and learned about my next destination. Even my dreams are filled with one thing and one thing only: *Alaska*.

OK. Maybe two things ...

Some of my nervous excitement might be related to Franco. Since closing the book on Andrew, I've opened my heart a bit wider to my Chilean travel buddy. We've talked about lots more than planning our trip by this point. He may still be guarded, but I've gotten to learn more about his childhood and upbringing. I can recognize that there's plenty he keeps hidden from me, but maybe a few days alone in the Alaskan outback will crack this tough nut open wide enough to get to the good stuff inside. (Sorry, that sounded way grosser than intended.)

Mom is anxious about the trip. Apparently the bears of Denali sound more threatening to her than James and Callie and the Jolly Orcas. Gary, who himself is an avid outdoorsman, has stood up to her on my behalf. He assured her that as long as we aren't stupidly storing food in our tents or trying to take selfies with their cubs, the bears couldn't be less interested in us.

She hasn't appreciated that side of him very much. Truth be told, she doesn't care much for *you* right now either.

But I'm 21, and she's powerless to stop me! Mwahahahaha! (It'll be all the irony when I *do* get eaten by a bear on the first night ...)

OK. Time to hit the hay. Big day tomorrow! I should have been in bed an hour ago.

Love, your (too-excited-to-sleep) little girl,
Kate

---------- FIVE ----------

Into the Storm

June 18, 2023

Dear Dad,

I've always hated window seats on airplanes. OK, they aren't quite as craptastic as middle seats, but you're still pretty squished in there like a sandwich at the bottom of a lunchbox. The only bright side of a window seat is that you don't have to get up whenever someone in your row has to take a piss.

Today, however, suffering the window seat was worth every cramped second of it. I didn't time exactly how long our jet skirted the coasts of British Columbia and southeast Alaska, and I'm not sure I could have. Every stopwatch in the world would have held its breath with me as I gazed down on a timeless world where towering emerald mountains meet and kiss the sea. Behind these, like aging parents standing at attention for their marrying children, were the white heads of the coastal Rockies' dominant peaks. More beauty hides down there than one person could see up close in a lifetime. But from six miles in the air, I can mine their treasures in only a couple hours.

By the time my Alaska Airlines flight landed in Anchorage, a sagging, exhausted sensation was creeping over me. I had been in the air for over five hours, but due to multiple time changes, it was barely one o'clock. Since Franco's plane wasn't supposed to touch down until after six sharp, I hailed a taxi to drive me to my hotel. No sooner had the vehicle left the airport loop than we found our roadway blocked by a behemoth bull moose.

That woke me up. I'm definitely in Alaska!

The redheaded cabbie, taking stock of my gaping jaw and saucer-sized eyeballs, wheezed a throaty smoker's laugh and said, "Know what we call that here?"

"What?" I naively replied.

"A Sunday afternoon!" he said, and followed his own pathetic punchline with a hearty belly laugh.

"Never been to Alaska before, have ya?"

"Nope. First time."

"Based on that spiffy blue backpack of yours, I'm guessing you're here for pleasure, not business," he asserted, scratching his scraggly salt-and-paprika beard. "Where ya headed?"

"Denali," I said. "Gonna spend a few days in the backcountry there."

"By yourself?" He asked the question as if I were a crazy woman.

"No," I assured him. "My friend is meeting me here."

"Ah. Got it."

The taxi went silent for a minute as the moose left and my driver navigated us toward downtown Anchorage. From my vantage point, Alaska's most populated city appeared only marginally larger than Cheyenne. There were a few taller buildings congregated together, but nothing higher than a handful of stories.

"When ya leavin'? For Denali?" the cab driver asked, breaking the quiet again.

"Tomorrow morning," I answered. "Renting a car and driving up."

He grunted with what I took to be disapproval, then cautioned, "Might wanna wait a few days. We're supposed to get some wicked weather sweeping down from the north. Ya don't wanna get caught out in the backcountry with that mess."

"Thanks for the tip!" I exclaimed politely, though I had no intention (and still have none) of postponing. After all, I have my certified mountain ranger coming along to keep me safe and sound!

Speaking of Franco ...

His flight arrived an hour later than expected. I had been sitting in front of the hotel TV, impatiently watching *Everybody Loves Raymond* reruns, when he texted to let me know wheels were on the tarmac. An annoying flutter of anticipation began winging about my stomach. I immediately told the butterflies inside me to calm down, but (as tummy butterflies are prone to do) they didn't listen one damn bit.

Franco's next text read: *I will pick up rental car and meet you at hotel. Good?*

He's 27. Much cheaper if the rental car is under his name.

Perfect! I wrote back. *We can find dinner and shop for our hiking supplies. SEE YOU SOON!*

I spent the next few minutes in front of the bathroom mirror, trying to turn my hair and makeup-less face into something more presentable. When I was still far from satisfied, I gave up and returned to the TV, but my mind was miles away from the Barone family arguing on the screen. My upcoming meeting with Franco occupied every cell and synapse in my brain. What would I say to Franco when I saw him? What he would say to me? Should I hug him? If so, for how long? Handshake? (Hell no, not a handshake.) Play it cool? Or admit how happy I was to see him in person again?

I sent another mental message to my squirming stomach (I think giant eels had eaten the butterflies and were now its new residents), telling it to settle the hell down. Its streak of rebellion continued, apparently unfazed by my will.

The next text from Franco didn't come until a full episode later: *Long line at the rental kiosk. Leaving now.*

Enter yet another period of strained waiting. At least the company changed. The Heffernan family from *King of Queens* had replaced *Raymond.*

Checking in, Franco informed by text near the end of the first episode. *What is your room number?*

I told him.

Perfecto. I will come down after shower and change.

Well, it was damn near 8:30 by the time that turd finally knocked. Forget hugging him or telling him how glad I was to see him. I wanted nothing more than to punch him for making me wait that long!

Nevertheless, I opened the door, and there he was. The same cockeyed grin. The same wavy espresso hair. The same chocolate-fondue eyes gazing down at me. The only difference between Torres Franco and Alaska Franco is that he (wisely) scraped off the scraggly beard. *Much* more handsome this way, if you ask me.

Franco stepped into my room, and then into me. He wrapped his arms around my back and held me against himself in a firm hug.

In that moment the eels residing in my stomach wriggled right up into my chest. I feared where they might move next.

"It is good to see you again, Kate," he said quietly, hesitantly, as he stepped back.

First he's late, then he steals my move and my line? Super turd!

But honestly, all I felt was happiness.

"Good to see you too, Franco!" I replied. "Wanna go get dinner? I'm starving."

"Absolutely!" he exclaimed. "I have not eaten in days, I feel."

Even though it was nearing nine o'clock, the sun remained in suspension above the horizon. A chilly, salted breeze ruffled our hair and clothing as we left the hotel and explored downtown Anchorage, hoping to spy out an eatery which would suit our raging appetites. We made small talk as we strolled: "How was the flight?" "I love this weather." "Anything would be fine for dinner." "But I do love seafood!" "Wonder where there's a decent grocery store around here to find our backpacking supplies?" Even though the conversation could only be called entirely unstimulating by an outside observer, I was content, at complete ease with him. I'm not always the greatest judge of what another person is thinking, but I'd gamble that he felt the same.

We finally settled on some brewhouse. Can't remember the name right now, but it provided me with outstanding ahi tuna. I insisted on paying ... and not just for dinner, but for the entire trip. (You left me so much, Dad, that generosity comes to me quite easily now!) Once dinner was finished, we returned to the hotel and took the rental car to Fred Meyer, which is basically a grocery store with a dash of Walmart added to the recipe. Here we bought mostly food: lots of noodle and rice dishes (which Franco says are light to carry and easy to cook), as well as granola bars, oatmeal for breakfast, and other snacky goodies for the in-between hours. We also picked up fuel for your gas stove, fresh first aid equipment, and a few other odds and ends. When Franco was satisfied our haul would sustain a four-day backcountry trip, he pushed our cart to the checkout lane. Here was where *he* insisted on paying, and he wouldn't take *no* for an answer.

"I must contribute something, Kate," he insisted. "Consider it my way of buying into your father's special trip."

Like that chocolate in his eyes, I almost melted.

Back at the hotel, we said goodnight. He went to his room. I went to mine.

Here I am now. It's past midnight. I wasn't even going to write to you. I just wanted to go to sleep, but right now that seems as impossible as a telepathic unicorn winning the lottery. I think I get excited too easily. It's a disease. We're supposed to leave after hotel breakfast around 7:30, but if this whole insomnia thing keeps up, I might have to push that timetable back an hour or two.

Maybe there's something decent on TV that'll put me under.

Anyway, I'll keep you updated as we make our way to Denali, and then to Anderson Pass. God willing, that's where I'll be sleeping two nights from now!

Love, your (insomniac) little girl,
Kate

June 19, 2023

Dear Dad,

I'm not sure which opening line is best for today's report, so I'll let you choose between my top two:

1. What the *hell* have you gotten me into?

OR

2. I wasn't even this cold above the Arctic Circle in *January!*

Maybe I should give you some context before you choose ...

The day started out a touch later than expected. At the time I figured it was no big deal. As it turns out, leaving Anchorage an hour later than planned was but the first tiny snowball sent rolling down a steep hill.

The drive north, as you're already aware, offered me and Franco one gorgeous vista after another. Even though I looked up our route beforehand, I can't believe how desolate the world is here. In a way, the drive to Denali reminded me sharply of the Patagonian wilds. Once past the town of Wasilla, there are about three gas stations, 250 miles of potholed pavement, fifty thousand mountains, and fifty billion trees. Yet in the desolation there also lives a beauty unlike anything built by humankind. What we sweat and strive together to create, nature surpasses without ever thinking about its labor.

Aaaaaaaaaand that's about where my positivity comes to an end.

By the time we arrived at the Denali National Park visitor center, we were already pushing one o'clock in the afternoon. The ranger who was supposed to be manning the backcountry office wasn't there when we showed up (something about a bear management situation), which meant we couldn't get the proper permits for backcountry camping until later.

No big deal, right? But the snowball rolls on, gaining both speed and size.

Shortly before three in the afternoon, the ranger returned. He explained to us the "backcountry unit" system, how the whole park is divided up into numbered zones. Each of those units, then, accommodates a certain number of campers per night. (I'm sure you're already familiar with the system, but just in case it's changed since the early 2000s, now you know.) Fortunately, the units leading to Anderson Pass still had their *VACANCY* signs illuminated. Once we had watched the mandatory safety video for backcountry campers, the ranger signed our permits. We had planned to begin our hike right where you told me, at the Mt. Eielson Visitor Center some sixty miles into the park, but Ranger Rick (yes, that was actually his name) convinced us that a launch point from Grassy Pass, only a short distance beyond, would trim away a good hour of hiking.

Our next job was to buy tickets for the shuttle. Since you can't drive personal vehicles very far down the park road, we had no choice but to ride the bus to our drop-off point. Unfortunately, when we arrived at the ticketing desk, we discovered that every bus seat was sold out until 4:30. But this is the land of the midnight sun, right? No big deal! Sure, we wouldn't arrive at our drop-off location until later in the evening, but Franco and I still believed everything would be fine and dandy. So we hung out. We talked. We played cards. We talked some more. I called Mom with his phone because mine was dead, then counted all the different ways one person could tell another to be careful. And, finally, we got on the shuttle and left.

When the rain began at 9:15, we were still onboard that shuttle. It wasn't an all-out downpour or anything. Rather, it was one of those lazy, chilled drizzles that's somehow *worse* than torrential rains. Fat, gray clouds hung over our heads, so near we could almost touch them. That was still the prevailing weather when our shuttle operator stopped at Grassy Pass, a short distance past the Eielson Visitor Center, to let us off. Then, with a snappy goodbye, he closed the door, sped away, and disappeared behind the rain veil.

I'll summarize the subsequent details, because I think I'm finally warm enough to fall asleep.

First, we descended down 500 feet of scree (you know, the steep slope of loose stones practically designed to roll ankles). Next came two miles across the gray, graveled flats of the many-braided Thorofare River. As a special treat, this section included five bridgeless river crossings through 32.1-degree glacial meltwater. We're lucky the drizzle hadn't dropped enough moisture to swell those streams, or else we would've been royally screwed. By the time we finally traversed the wide riverbed, midnight had come and gone, and we still hadn't crossed inside the boundaries of our permitted camping unit. That relief would only belong to us after another hour of hiking south along Glacier Creek, a meager waterway pinned between the imposing Mt. Eielson on one side and low hills of glacial moraine on the other.

Once Franco determined that we had crossed the proper zone's boundary, we found a flat deposit of glacial silt, threw our tents together in silence, stowed our bear proof food container a good distance away (as you're well aware, you don't want to attract 500-pound grizzlies into your sleeping quarters), and crawled inside our damp sleeping bags. We're both hungry, but sleep is winning out tonight. Dinner will have to wait until breakfast. That's how exhausted, cold, and miserable we are.

Dad, this next letter of yours better be a frickin' Newbery Medal winner, or else I might give up looking for the rest of them. I mean it.

Love, your (food-and-sleep-starved) little girl,
Kate

June 20, 2023

Dear Dad,

Franco woke me up this morning, frantic with excitement. Something more must have gone wrong, I was certain of it. Surely some clever critter had figured out how to pick the locks on our bear proof canister and eaten all our food. Or perhaps an army of irate grizzlies was descending upon us from the higher slopes, surrounding our camp, ravenous and craving human flesh.

"What is it?" I cried back to Franco, my panicked mind groping through the fog of sleep and lingering fatigue.

"Just come out here!" he pleaded. "You must see this, Kate."

Abundant sunshine and crisp, dewy air cascaded upon my bare face as I stuck my head out from the road-stripe-yellow tent. Above me loomed the hulking shadow of what I knew must be Mt. Eielson. The nasty weather my cabbie warned me about had now passed. When it came and went, it had apparently scrubbed away with it everything impure or dull or ugly. Only the pristine loveliness of untouched Alaska remained.

But Franco was uninterested in what had captivated my attention. Already he was walking westward toward the grassy, low-lying mounds of glacial upheaval, heather-green and boulder-strewn.

Over his shoulder he called, "Not that. Follow me!"

After a quick wrestling match with my North Face fleece, I crammed my sore and blistered feet into the damp hiking boots I'd left overnight beneath the tent's rain fly. Without even bothering to lace up, I stumbled out and after Franco, who was scrambling up the steep hill. Once on top, he stopped next to a Buick-sized boulder and leaned against it.

I too crested the high mound.

There, my heart caught in my throat. Spread out before us, stretching for countless miles, was a tapestry so magnificent, God himself would be blessed to hang it in his throne room. Threads of glaciers, rivers frozen in time, were woven among mountains blue and purple and green and orange. And, enthroned above it all, the radiant crown which not a cloud dared obscure, stood the King of kings among all North America's mighty peaks.

Denali itself. Surrounded by the lesser spires of the Alaska Range. A royal court bowing low before its ruler.

"Incredible," murmured Franco, transfixed.

Several minutes we stood, silent but for our breathing in and out. Then, unexpectedly, Franco slipped a hand around my shoulder and pulled me into his side. My exhilaration, already formidable, was suddenly big as Denali itself. I allowed myself to lean into him, and there we stood, an improbable pair brought together through an unusual series of events. Events set in motion by you, Dad. For those brief moments, at least, the world was right.

They were also the moments when I realized, without a doubt, that I was in love with Franco. Not even the stars of heaven or the bedrock beneath my feet were as substantial as this epiphany. It slammed into me with all the force of a semi-truck barreling into a butterfly. I sucked in new breath, deeper and sweeter, then again, and again, as if I'd lived in a cave my whole life and were being introduced to fresh air for the first time. Everything—my world, my entire existence—had changed forever.

Until now, I've always found creepy the popular idea that girls fall for guys like their dads. In Franco's case, though, I begrudgingly have to admit it might be true. Like you, he has an unquenchable thirst for adventure. He's introspective and genuine. He speaks to me the way you write to me, as if I'm the only thing in the world that matters. Even beyond the direct similarities I see between the two of you, Franco is passionate and funny. He loves to laugh and is nearly always smiling. He cares about our earth, both for its wild wonders and for the people who walk it. In short, there's very little *not* to love, so I would be crazy to feel differently.

Dammit, Emma, I hate it when you're right ...

I know. It was quick, especially after all the Andrew stuff that went down only a few months ago. But I also know it is real. I don't know *how* I know, only that I do.

And that, I suppose, is enough.

I have no sense of how long we stood together, eyes feasting on the captivating beauty which encompassed us. The stream of time, in places like that, has a way of flowing differently. On its silvery waters a minute might be an hour, and an hour a minute. Whichever it was, I do not know. All I know is that the power of Denali, and of Franco, and of life, held us rooted there in silence, magnetized both to the earth and to each other.

Eventually, the rumblings of an even more powerful force, our un-dinnered and un-breakfasted stomachs, tore us away from the image, and we descended back down the glacial moraine to our tents.

A quiet breakfast of instant oatmeal followed. We chitchatted about the misery of the previous night and counted our blessings that today, by all appearances, would be more agreeable. We broke down our tents, replaced our gear snugly into our backpacks, and continued south along the creek. Our bodies, still in recovery mode, needed lunch after only an hour or so of hiking. As we ate granola bars and trail mix, our mealtime entertainment arrived in the form of a wolverine pair scuffling upon a nearby slope. Whether they were playing or fighting, we'll never know. After a few minutes, the duo scuttled over the ridge and out of sight.

Throughout the early part of the afternoon, we hiked onward. The further we went, the fiercer the winds sweeping down from the higher elevations became. Eventually, around three o'clock, we arrived at the terminus of a gently sloping creek bed. Towering ahead now was the steep climb up Anderson Pass. The winds, continuing only to grow stronger, launched gales of dust and even tiny stones into our faces, a million minuscule missiles, assaulting us in waves of ceaseless barrage.

"I do not think we should climb today," Franco opined after we set down our packs for what I assumed was only a break. "The wind and sand will blind us before we reach the pass. Things will be calmer in the morning."

As excited as I am to read your letter, I didn't hate his suggestion. The idea of a relaxed evening spent exploring the surrounding terrain appealed to me. The lunchtime wolverine wrestling match had sparked the fires of curiosity within me, and I wondered what other wildlife encounters we might enjoy if we stayed put for a while.

Since it's been too blustery to set up our tents thus far, I decided I'd write to you a little earlier than usual. Right now I'm sitting, all alone, in the lee of a boulder on the hillside. Even though a curtain of clouds has veiled the glory of Denali, much of this morning's topographical tapestry remains spread before me. I have no idea where Franco wandered off, but it doesn't matter. I like that we can enjoy our own adventures beyond the reach of each other's shadows.

You know, last night I wanted to kill you dead all over again. I was miserable and cold and ready to throw in the towel. I'm glad I pushed on. I'm glad your letters *keep* pushing me on. Because if I had given up anywhere along the way, or if you had given up during your last days, the course of my life would never have included this. Though I may not have known what was missing, my heart would have always carried within it a Denali-sized hole.

And that's a pretty damn big piece! I'm glad I got to fill it today.

Alright … better go down to start dinner and set up camp. In the morning we climb, and, if all goes well, I'll have your letter filling another piece of my heart by this time tomorrow.

Love, your (completely content) little girl,
Kate

July 9th, 2003

Dear Kate—

Here is where it all began. In a way, I have this place to thank for my whole life.

I had just graduated high school when I came to Alaska the first time. Both my parents were still alive then. We lived in the university town of Manhattan, Kansas, where your grandparents were professors at Kansas State (Go Wildcats!), an impressive feat, given the fact both of them were tenured there before the age of forty.

During the course of my final high school semester, a trio of baseball friends and I decided to travel to Alaska for a week of fishing and sightseeing. As graduation drew nearer, however, they all dropped out one by one. Jimmy cited money as the reason he couldn't go. Carl had to work. Dom blamed his controlling girlfriend, who wouldn't let him leave her for such a long time.

I never was one to let others ruin my fun just because they decided to be lame idiots, so I decided to visit Alaska on my own. My parents weren't the adventurous, live-outside-the-box types themselves, but they almost always supported even my craziest decisions—regardless of whether said decisions weren't thought out very well.

Long story short, my final plan for the trip led me here, to Denali. It wasn't just my first solo backpacking trip. It was my *first backpacking trip.* Period. And I had chosen for my inaugural expedition the many-grizzlied, trailless, bridge-free wilderness of a park the size of Massachusetts!

It was intimidating. It was tough. At times it was downright miserable.

It was beautiful. It was inspiring. It was *wild.*

Suddenly, my entire previous life felt sheltered, even tame by comparison. I had grown up a domesticated lapdog. A wolf is what I became on that trip.

It was here, atop Anderson Pass, on a cloudless, crisp, magnificent morning, when my greatest epiphany struck me. I saw in a moment what I would do for the rest of my life: travel, then write about those travels. I would become friend to both the wild places of the world and its teeming cities. Like a snake sheds its skin, I would shrug off my groomed, comfortable life and adopt the wandering way of the wolf.

When I returned home to Kansas, I changed nearly every plan I had made. It only took a week to withdraw my college enrollment, pack my well-bruised Oldsmobile Firenza, and leave Manhattan.

Was it risky? Absolutely. Uncertain? You bet. Did the decision piss off my parents? Royally. Even the most supportive ones have their limits. It was also one of the bravest, boldest, and best decisions of my entire life. Pursuing my passion rather than settling for a relatively riskless career in an office was, perhaps, the defining moment of my entire existence.

For months I explored as much of our country as I could find. When I wanted nature, I camped among the redwoods of California or the Saguaros of Arizona. When I wanted company, I meandered San Antonio's Riverwalk or Beale Street in Memphis. I studied. I read. I learned. And I wrote. Everything I saw, everything I experienced, I inked into my journals.

Before too long, my freelance pieces began appearing in periodicals and magazines. The money wasn't great in the beginning, but it kept me moving. I was hungry sometimes, but I didn't care.

I was happy. I was *alive.*

Kate, my daughter—my chubby, cuddly, crack-me-up daughter—examine your heart. What path are you on? What road are you following, and toward what horizon? If you continue in that direction, where will you end up? Who will you become? Someone you love? Someone you admire? Or someone you're ashamed to see staring back at you in the mirror?

I have no way of discovering which passions will overtake your beating heart, or what work you will consider worth doing. But whatever they are, whatever it is you most believe will give you purpose, whatever will rouse you from bed in the morning filled with excitement to greet each new day—I pray with all my heart you spend your life doing exactly that and settling for nothing less.

That's how you live wild. That's how you live free.

This world already has far too many in its domesticated herds. They wander through their bucolic motions each day, safe behind their fences, lazily meandering through the same pastures. They are people existing as hollow shells and faint shadows of what they might have been, had they but broken down those fences of their own making to seize what lay beyond. Your Dada wants better for you than that kind of soul-killing existence.

So live wild, Kate. Live free.

I so wish I could be there to help guide you along your way. But I'm not. And that means it is up to you. Find what sets your heart ablaze and put your ass to work building one hell of a bonfire.

By the time you finish reading these words of mine, you'll have reached the halfway point of my adventures for you. I wish, of course, there could be a thousand left. There's so much more I want to say, so many corners of my heart I wish I could show you.

Time, though, is waning, as is my energy. They are the wax and wick of a candle, and here at the twilight of my day, I am quickly spending both with my brightly burning flame. Yet somehow, I am certain I'll find the strength required to finish what I started. Only this time it won't be my passion for travel or writing pressing me onward, sustaining me to accomplish what I set out to do. Now I have an even greater passion driving me toward the finish line.

I have you, Kate. And that means I will have all the strength I need.

I love you now and always,
Dad

Your next destination should pair nicely with this one, as long as you have the time. From Alaska you'll travel south along the Pacific coast to Washington. Here you will find Rialto Beach. It isn't one of the gaudy, bikini-sprinkled, sandy shores you're probably familiar with, but one whose polychronic floor is paved with sea-polished stones. The bleached bones of giant Sitka spruce trees litter its landscape like the inside of a dragon's cave.

The beach lies west of Forks, Washington. When you arrive there, make your way north along the coast, but not too far. Perhaps a half-mile up the beach, a trio of massive logs forms a sort of leaning teepee at the edge of the forest. They're so large and lodged in place that I doubt whether they'll have moved, not even twenty years from now.

Using those logs as your starting point, walk directly into the woods about thirty feet. There you'll find a triangular, moss-covered boulder, a four-foot-tall wedge of petrified cake. Directly below the point of that cake rock is where you need to dig. If you burrow far enough, you'll find another lockbox just like the one at your grandparents' and the one I am about to bury here at Anderson Pass. As was the case with this one, you won't need a key to open it.

In case you're having trouble finding it, or if my landmarks aren't where I left them, use the GPS coordinates listed on the backside of this page.

Do me one favor: read the letter at sunset.

Be safe, and happy hunting!

P.S. If you have some extra time, check out the tide pools near the sea stacks here—anemones and starfish and urchins galore! It's pretty wild!

June 21, 2023

Dear Dad,

Did you have a theme in mind whilst organizing the locations of your scavenger hunt?

If so, was that theme word *COLD?*

Today is the summer solstice, the longest day of the entire year. I'd been looking forward to it, ready to watch the sun swing around the sky without setting until well after midnight.

Now I'm just trying to survive the day. Literally.

Remember when my cab driver warned me about a front of nasty weather moving down from the north? I assumed that's what hit us a couple nights ago when we began our backpacking trip. I figured the clear skies yesterday morning meant that we also were in the clear.

I couldn't have been more wrong.

This morning we woke up to much the same conditions as last night. The wind, however, had shifted at some point, so that it was blowing steadily from the north. None of this raised any alarms for either me or Franco. If anything, the herd of caribou meandering by as I unzipped my tent door this morning came as an encouragement, an auspicious forecasting of a dazzling day in Denali.

We ate. We packed. We commenced our arduous trudge up the slopes toward the pass.

Within an hour, the azure canopy overhead had turned the color of campfire ash. The wind grew swifter and steadier and colder, the temperature plummeting harder than Lindsay Lohan's career. A darkness, unnatural for the time of day, settled over the sun until it was extinguished like a candle beneath a snuffer.

"Do you think we should turn back?" I shouted to Franco above the gale.

He shook his head. "We are closer to the top than to the bottom," he explained. "Once there, we can set up our tents and weather the storm. I also do not think we want to be near the creek bed if it starts to flood."

I was worried we wouldn't gain the pass before the rain began, but our luck held a little longer. Shortly past noon, and still dry, we scaled the slope's final ascent and seized the broad saddle of Anderson Pass. Without hesitating to rest or rehydrate, we put up our tents and staked them into the rocky earth as best we could, taking care to weigh down the interior corners with stones and items from our packs. Since there was no precipitation *yet,* I went to work hunting for the circular array of stones you mentioned in your letter.

Less than three minutes later, I found the landmark. It appeared untouched, two decades old since its creation. I dug down with my poophole shovel (because what the hell else am I gonna call the shovel I use to bury my own crap?). A minute later I was scraping metal. To me, it was pay dirt.

"Hurry inside!" I heard Franco call above the storm. "I see the line of rain coming at us!"

With all the urgency of a hunted gopher, I excavated the box. Once it was liberated from its long imprisonment, I tucked it beneath my arm, ran back to my tent, and zipped the door shut literal seconds before the deluge began its furious knocking. Panting from the frenzied effort of the last few minutes, I let myself rest. Only once my breathing had slowed did I finally move the lockbox from armpit to lap. I wiped the caked dirt away from the latch and opened it.

Sealed against the elements in quadruple Ziploc bags was your letter, now seeing the light of day for the first time in twenty years.

I read it. I read it again, and then a third time.

I give it a B+. Definitely not the Newbery winner I was hoping for. "Living wild like a wolf ... following paths and roads ... heart like a bonfire." Pick a damn metaphor and stick with it, Dad! Jeez ... weren't you supposed to be a professional writer?

Maybe I'm just a bit cranky with you right now. After all, as I write this I'm beginning to wonder if it'll be *my* last letter to *you.*

You see, the rain didn't stay rain for long. About a half hour after starting, it turned to snow. Every ten minutes for the last four hours, Franco and I have been clearing our tent roofs, so the snow doesn't cave them in and crush us. A wall five inches deep has already piled up around the tent bases, and the skies show no signs of relenting. We are under siege, holed up in our flimsy castles, cut off from retreat, and praying our old ally the sun shows up to drive the enemy away.

Maybe this was your idea all along: lure me here, capture me, kill me. Then I'll join you up there, and you won't be all alone anymore.

A clever, meticulously executed plan, Dad.

Well, let me tell you something ... I love you. But I'm not ready to die. I'm not ready to be with you yet. So you're gonna have to wait a while. Please? If you're on good terms with whoever has the power to turn on and off the weather, maybe you could put in a little plea for me and Franco.

Time to clear off the tent again. I do hope this won't be my final letter to you.

Love, your (never-been-scared-er) little girl,
Kate

June 25, 2023

Dear Dad,

Thanks for all the help ...

After I last wrote you, the world sank deeper into the dark and cold and snow. The condensation inside our tents started to freeze. The frost settled down into our sleeping bags, then into our bodies. We were eventually so cold that Franco joined me in my smaller tent. Once our sleeping bags were zipped together, we could at least share our warmth like hibernating bears.

For over a day we lived like this, taking turns dozing because he was worried if we both nodded off, the snow would flatten the tent and suffocate us.

"What should we do?" I asked at one point through chattering teeth. The ubiquitous, gray shroud spread end to end across the sky made it impossible to tell the time of day.

Franco pulled me against himself and said, "We pray, and we wait."

"You don't think we should leave? Try to get back to that visitor center?"

I sensed him shaking his head. "No," he said. "That would be even more dangerous than staying put. This blizzard cannot last forever. Soon it will warm up, and we will be safe to travel then."

"What if it doesn't?" I asked, my cynical side now the exclusive voice within me.

"I would not leave here," he reiterated, "unless it were a clear difference between life and death."

We talked, of course, as we waited. Perhaps weakened by cold and hunger, I finally divulged to him the whole dramatic tale of me and Andrew. He, in turn, shared tales of the Patagonian wilds and interesting or famous travelers he had met there. We both unveiled dreams we had for the future, where we saw ourselves in five years, and in ten. When we weren't talking, we slept in shifts. My fingers were too numb to write, so I read. On and on the hours dragged, the dull light eventually succumbing to night's shade for a brief time, only for the dull light to return shortly thereafter.

As disastrous as our trip had already been, disaster was but beginning to bare its bloodthirsty teeth.

In the early morning of the blizzard's third day, it went for the jugular. Our stomachs were empty (we hadn't eaten since lunchtime the day before), so Franco volunteered to fetch the bear proof food container stashed a short distance from our tents. After bundling himself in all the clothes he'd brought, he set out to retrieve it from the foot of the rock where it was stored.

Five minutes passed. Then ten. Maybe more. I think I dozed off. But Franco didn't come back. I called out to him, praying harder than Jonah in the whale, not so much for his safety, but so that I wouldn't have to leave my marginally warmer sleeping bag to peek outside.

He didn't answer.

When I finally worked up the willpower to emerge from my synthetic cocoon, I learned why. About a hundred feet away, next to our food storage boulder and partially buried under the wet snow, a body lay flat on the ground.

Usain Bolt couldn't have run faster than I did, shoeless through the snow. Collapsing beside him, I grabbed his shoulders and shook. A soft moan escaped his purple lips and sent a wave of relief crashing over me. But, as with any wave, it promptly retreated, leaving bare panic behind. There, blossoming in the snow beneath his head, was a crimson bloom of blood. My best guess is that he slipped backward upon reaching the food canister, and that his fall was broken by an ice-glazed stone.

So was the back of his skull.

I don't know how I managed to drag him back inside the tent. I must have channeled my inner Schwarzenegger or something, like those moms who lift cars off their trapped babies. Anyway, I wrapped him tightly against myself in the sleeping bag, willing what little warmth I possessed out of my body and into his. Fortunately, he hadn't been immersed in the elements too long. His own body heat returned, slowly but fully.

The real problem, I then realized, wasn't hypothermia. It was his head. Concussion? Definitely. Blood loss? Duh. Fractured skull and swelling around the brain? Likely.

I'm no nurse, but flashes of first aid training from my high school lifeguarding days revisited me. After practically ripping a zipper off your backpack, I retrieved your first aid kit and tore it open. Inside I located a gauze wrap. Propping him into a semi-seated position against his backpack was small potatoes compared to dragging him through the snow. Now, with better access to his head, I was able to wrap a firm compress around his skull. Sure, a true nurse would have enjoyed a good laugh at my handiwork, but it was the best I could provide under the circumstances. I decided next to give him something for the pain. In the emergency kit, I located a foil packet containing an individual serving of aspirin. Unsure if he would swallow it in his catatonia, and not wanting him to choke, I placed the pair of tablets on his tongue and splashed them with a capful of water. To my immense relief, Franco's reflexes took over, and he swallowed the pills.

My relief was once again short-lived. Seconds later, it was engulfed by terror.

In my haste, I hadn't been thinking things through. If I had maintained control over my wits, I might have remembered that *aspirin is a blood thinner.* I had just given a profusely bleeding man pills that would make his bleeding *even worse.* Franco's life was placed in my hands, and instead of saving him, I had pulled the lever to drop the guillotine.

I weighed my options, but not for long. There was only one road remaining at that point. Franco had told me he wouldn't leave the tent to hike back unless it meant the difference between life and death ...

In my previous letter, I told you I thought I might die. When I left that tent with nothing warmer than a North Face fleece and windbreaker, death seemed like a guarantee. But I couldn't lie there and do nothing while Franco bled out or his brain hemorrhaged. I couldn't cradle his limp body in my arms and merely *hope* my colossal screw-up wouldn't kill him. The situation required action, so action was what I gave it.

I'm pretty sure I caught sight of the Grim Reaper trailing after me as I half-stumbled, half-slipped my way down the vertical quarter mile from Anderson Pass. Mere minutes into my solo expedition, I was ninety percent certain my toes were either frozen solid or had gone missing entirely. At the same time, a strangely warm pain in my nose and fingers made me wonder if the wind and snow were, in fact, laced with acid.

Mercifully, by the time I reached the lower altitudes of Glacier Creek's riverbed, the gale had slackened into a steady breeze. There was also less snow and ice here, which meant I could move at a turtle's pace instead of a snail's.

Every sense of time abandoned me as I crept northward toward the park road and the Mt. Eielson Visitor Center. I was conscious only of a driving and desperate need to exhaust every last calorie of energy I possessed. Streams crossed my path, and I plodded through without stopping to assess their risk. When I finally did encounter a grizzly, I gave it a wide berth and tramped on, unfazed. And, hours later, when my jelly legs needed to carry me six hundred feet up a steep slope, I didn't miss a beat until I was at the top and staring straight ahead at the visitor center.

The logical part of me has no explanation whatsoever for how I managed to finish that journey from Anderson Pass. My clothing was woefully inadequate, my stomach queasy with emptiness, and my body already half-frozen when I began. And yet, despite reason's inability to explain why I'm not dead in the snow, I know the answer. I know what kept me going.

It was *my* passion. It was Franco.

Just as your love for me, Dad, pushed you to finish the scavenger hunt, my love for Franco kept driving me forward through the storm, even when forward no longer seemed possible. As I stumbled toward the visitor center, shouting for help, I understood that my own life was inseparably bound to the one hanging in the balance on Anderson Pass. If I were going to live—truly *live* the way you described in your letter—it meant Franco had to live also.

For a short moment, when I reached the building's front entrance, I felt that life slip from my grasp.

The doors were closed. Locked. A handwritten sign I hadn't previously seen informed me that the building was closed due to weather. For a fraction of a moment, the emptiness of abject despair, magnified by my physical exhaustion, swallowed me down into oblivion.

Then I heard a voice, the gruff tones of a green-and-khaki-clad angel, shouting, "What's going on? What's wrong?"

It turns out there is a small ranger dormitory located around the west side of the visitor center. From within it, somehow, in some miraculous way, a lone park serviceman heard my pleas over the howling wind.

He brought me inside. He heard my frantic story. He radioed for help.

The helicopter pilot I spoke with late last night told me it was the worst weather he's ever flown in. More than once he felt certain everyone on-board had punched their one-way tickets to the afterlife.

But they made it to Anderson Pass and found Franco. He was in worse shape than when I'd left him, but alive. They airlifted him to a medical clinic in Healy, just north of the park's main entrance. Because I was unable to travel via the snow-covered road, all I could do was sit in agony and wait for news.

Eight minutes before midnight, Ranger Doug and I finally received that news: Franco had survived. He was still under intensive care, but doctors said his condition was stable.

Less than a minute later, I was asleep. The reward for my bravery and bitter labor was the deepest slumber of my entire life. Waves of unadulterated peace washed my weary mind of all its worry.

I awakened the next morning to clearing skies and only the faintest of breezes. Because of the sheer amount of snow covering the park road, I wasn't able to leave until the following day. Ranger Doug, snowbound as well, was kind enough between his long stints of clearing and salting the walkways to provide me with the periodic updates he received about Franco. Meanwhile, I sat contentedly and lazily in the ranger dormitory, watching normal colors return to my mildly frostbitten fingers between episodes of Doug's *Cheers* DVDs.

That evening, after a dinner of hot dogs, macaroni, and baked beans (Doug sure knows how to treat a lady right!), as the ranger was teaching me how to play a card game called cribbage, another of my worries was put to bed. I had assumed all our gear left at Anderson Pass would remain there, a monument to our failed expedition. Someday, I imagined, someone would pick up this very journal, with your letters stuffed inside the back cover, and piece together the partial love story of a dead dad and his little girl. As it turns out, Fate decided to intervene in the form of a park ecological cleanup crew.

So, thanks to an admirable and ambitious wilderness protection mentality, I was told our things would be waiting for us at the park's backcountry office.

Midmorning today, after a long and relaxing drive east along the park highway, I was able to pick them up. I fished the car keys from Franco's backpack and followed another ranger's directions to the meager hospital caring for my blizzard-battered companion.

He was sound asleep when I entered the room. The on-duty nurse brought me the most comfortable chair she could find. Except for a brief hiatus to eat, I've been here ever since. The hospital staff is keeping him sedated, but he did come to for a few hazy moments about an hour ago. It wasn't much. His eyelids fluttered as he offered a weak grin and gave my hand a reassuring squeeze.

Then, before slipping back into his drug-induced oblivion, he whispered, "You took me along because you thought you might need me. As it turns out, *I* am the one who needs *you.*"

I don't know if you were watching over me, Dad. I've always thought those ideas about the dead protecting their loved ones to be worth about as much as Blockbuster stock today. But in case you *were* watching over us, I want to say thanks. Not so much for taking care of me, but for taking care of the man who means the world to me.

Love, your (frostbitten) little girl,
Kate

June 26, 2023

Dear Dad,

I've always found the expression "a taste of one's own medicine" to be a little strange. After all, medicine heals and helps, yet the phrase carries with it a decidedly *negative* connotation. Regardless of my personal opinions about the saying, I guess it's the right one to describe what happened today. Everything began with the words that woke me up this morning.

"Hello, Kate," Franco murmured.

I jolted awake on my chair-bed. For a split second, I didn't remember where I was or how I'd gotten there. When the events of the previous days flooded into my consciousness, I jerked about and found Franco's coffee-bean eyes staring up at me. His color had returned, and, except for a bandage on his head and hair matted from his long sleep, he appeared strong and healthy.

Whatever spirit overtook me in that moment, I don't know. Maybe it was the resurgence of unimaginable relief. Maybe it was something else. But every restraint upon my heart broke free in that hospital room as I threw myself over him and pressed my lips against his.

Franco returned the impromptu kiss. My intense longing for him was reciprocated by his for me. At once, a waterfall began foaming inside my chest, and I felt as if everything might come bursting out all at once. Heat filled my cheeks, my fingers, my ears, my lips. It's possible I began to glow.

And it all lasted ... for about a second. Then Franco broke the connection. He averted his eyes and turned his face away from me. I backed off immediately and slumped into my chair.

"What is it? Franco, what's wrong?" I asked, confused, perhaps even a bit panicked over this abrupt change.

"I think," Franco replied, "that I should bring you back to Anchorage as soon as they let me leave here. Then you can go to Washington without me, and I will stay in Alaska."

That rushing waterfall remained in my chest, only now it was drowning me.

"But—huh? I don't get it," I stuttered. Frustration rose from my breast and into my throat. "Wasn't that your plan anyway? To stay longer in Alaska? Why are you being so weird?"

"I just ... I do not think you and I should ... be together," he said. "I think it is best if we go our separate ways from here."

"Look," I retorted angrily, "I'm sorry I kissed you just now. I guess I was relieved to see you conscious again. I spent almost a whole day certain you were gonna die. I thought we were *both* gonna die. It's been an emotional few days. That's all."

Franco sighed. "No. That is not all."

"The hell are you talking about?"

"I am sorry," he said sheepishly. "I should not have done this, but I ... I read from your book. Your words to your father."

Egregious, burning betrayal ripped through my gut. Teeth clenched, I growled, "That's personal, Franco. Between me and my dad." Then, adding a barb: "Or between me and no one, I guess, since he's *dead.*"

"Yes. I know. But when I woke up in that tent, you were gone. I had no memory of what happened. I likewise believed you were probably dead and that I would soon be joining you."

I held my stubborn glare. No way was I giving him the satisfaction of softening up for even a moment.

"It does not matter *why* I read your book," he continued. "What matters is that I know how you feel about me, and ... I cannot let myself feel that way about you."

The June 20 entry. Shit. Up to the moment of Franco's reminder, I'd forgotten how I stupidly shared that juicy little tidbit with you. I always knew being too open with my feelings would bite me in the ass sooner or later. Now I have proof.

But I wasn't ready to give up. Not without a fight.

"Well, why can't you?" I challenged, recalling his long emails, how he'd pulled me close to himself that first clear morning in Denali, and most recently, the obvious desire in the initial moment of our kiss. Could I really have been so foolish as to imagine love and longing where there had, in fact, been none at all?

"Some things are too difficult for explanation," Franco replied, risking a glance in my direction. "So, please, do not make me try. The time has come for us to walk our separate paths."

I stood. Turned to leave. Turned back again to face Franco. Stinging tears blurred his image as, bitterly, I whispered, "You told me you needed me. Last night when you woke up. You said *you* were the one who needs *me.* That was nothing?"

Franco's brow furrowed, and he again averted his gaze from mine. He wanted to say something, to explain himself, but the words eluded him.

He shook his head, defeated, and replied, "All I can say is that I am sorry, Kate. It would not be right."

As if yanked backward through time, I teleported to January, when Andrew sat where I find myself now. He was in love with me, yet I rejected him for reasons of my own that I couldn't explain. Did he hurt like I hurt now? Had his guts and innards and vital organs been ripped out, thrown into a blender, and whipped into an emotional smoothie? Because that's the consistency of mine right this very moment.

The bitter medicine I fed Andrew six months ago is precisely what I taste now.

No longer am I standing in a hospital room in Healy. I'm in Anchorage, all alone in my hotel room, still smelling the diesel fumes of the ancient bus that brought me here. Franco's image hovers in the darkness above my eyes, even as he lies in a hospital bed two hundred miles away.

I'm so angry. So dejected. So sad. And so damn tired. Yet sleep will not come. The specter of Franco scares it off every time it comes near.

Part of me wants to quit your game. The pain it has caused me—that *you* have caused me—overshadows and overwhelms the joy and wonder of it. You've led me to some amazing places and incredible people, sure. But before you showed up again, Dad, life was so much stabler and far less chaotic.

I want it done. Over. Finished.

So then ... why do I have a flight booked to Seattle? I leave early tomorrow afternoon. In my confusion and bitterness, I can't make sense of anything right now, not even my own decisions. I guess I'm forcing myself to act in the faith that pleasant shores are waiting over the horizon, even when the foaming waters around me are so turbulent and the night so deeply dark.

Like you did, I have to press onward. What other choice do I have? I'm too close to the finish line to quit the race now.

Besides, I really can't sink any lower than this, so one more letter won't hurt ... right?

Love, your (heartshattered) little girl,
Kate

---------- SIX ----------

Finding What We've Lost

July 4th, 2003

Dear Kate—

Maybe you were already aware, but your mom and I visited this very beach during our honeymoon. We were giddy children as we played among the tidepools and sea stacks and sun-bleached carcasses of giant Sitka spruce logs, washed to sea long ago down the rivers of the Olympic rainforest. That evening we sat breathlessly on this rocky shore, fingers intertwined, as soft ocean breezes teased our hair and an amber sun sank into the vast Pacific.

There were no deadlines, no mundane tasks looming over us. It was one of those rare nights when the world was pure, concentrated *wonder.* I remember thinking, even then, that I had not felt such a stirring for a long, long time. Truth be told, as I gaze back on that memory, the same sense of wonder would not revisit me for a long time after.

What happens to us? When we are very small, it seems there is nothing which cannot captivate us with wonder. When we are old, it seems there is nothing which *can.* To the toddler, every leaf, every bug, every color, every game mesmerizes and fills with delight. To the grown man, a night sky burning with its myriad stars or a valley surrounded by cathedral mountains has only the meagerest chance of accomplishing the same. Even what we adults obsess over and claim to love, whether sports or spouse or hobbies or music, only infrequently sows and grows within us the same sense of thrilling wonder which we can hardly escape as children!

When does it slip away? Where do we go wrong during the course of our lives that we lose something as precious as wonder? Perhaps some can point to a specific instance or source of trauma as their reason, but in the case of the average American adult, what horrible events could possibly rob us of such a vital piece of our souls?

After our evening on Rialto Beach, I spent many restless nights trying to wrestle down an answer. Perhaps our growing list of responsibilities chips imperceptibly away at the foundations of our wonder. Maybe countless smaller traumas and disappointments gobble it up in a billion tiny bites, termites in the framework of our spirits. In the end, though, none of the explanations I fabricated seemed satisfactory.

To this day, I still don't know the answer. Our gradual loss of wonder remains, to me, an unsolvable mystery.

I may not know the source of the disease. But, as far as my life is concerned, I know the medicine.

The cure was you, Kate. The day you came into my world, wonder again became a part of my everyday existence (along with about a million crap-streaked diapers). While your tiny self stared for an hour, hypnotized, at something as simple as a caterpillar, I would gaze that whole time in amazement at you. Life took on a fresh flavor, as if seasoned with a never-before-tasted spice, simply because you had become a part of it. Every day I woke up wondering what glorious rays of sunshine and beauty you might radiate into my world.

It is my hope now, as I write this letter and bury it in the earth, that I might give back what you gave me: the gift of rediscovered wonder.

I'm no psychic, but I do know life will beat you to a bloody pulp in as many ways as it can. It will break your heart. It will dangle your dreams just out of reach. It will steal and destroy pieces of your world you believed you could never live without. I'm not trying to sound pessimistic. I'm being *realistic.* Nobody leads a charmed life, and nobody is untouchable. In short, life can be a real dick sometimes.

That is precisely the reason why a sense of wonder is so important, Kate. When life's innumerable troubles wound us, when the daily disappointments leave us deeply scarred, it is wonder which rescues us and pulls our teetering souls back from the brink. In a world where so much has gone and will go bad, it is our sense of wonder which reminds us there is even more that is bright and fresh and lovely. You just have to keep your eyes open. You must see and remember the light around you, even during—*especially* during—the days which appear as dark as night.

In ways I would never wish upon my worst enemies, that is the lesson I've learned these past months. When I found out I was sick—fatally so—dark clouds crowded around me. More than once I was sure they would swallow me whole and leave me in despair. But you, Kate, more than anything else, are the one who kept them at bay. Even during what can only be described as the worst of times, I have not lost my sense of wonder because my blond, ocean-eyed little girl is with me every single day. Smiling at me. Laughing with me. Reminding me constantly that this world is, and always will be, a wonderful, wonder-filled place.

Thank you for helping me reclaim what I lost. I treasure it every waking moment. Even now, in these final hours before the sunset of my life, that wonder sustains me. Soon, it will lead me into the darkness.

And then beyond.

Now, for you, the sun is also sinking into its watery bed at the end of its long day (unless you're a rebellious daughter who decided *not* to read this at sunset, as per my instructions). It also means evening is falling on this particular leg of your travels. You've successfully found five of my letters.

Only two remain. As you put the final pieces of my puzzle into place, I pray that the completed picture will plant the seed of wonder in your heart.

Growing, then blossoming there, may it never die.

I love you now and always,
Dad

Take some time now to recharge and regroup. Go and see your mom. Remind her how much I love her ... how much I always will. Then, when you're ready, make your way to the town of Lucca in Italy. This Tuscan city is one of the few remaining which still has its Renaissance-era wall encircling it. Once there, head north beyond the wall along the Via per Camaiore. You will come, before too long, to a narrow bridge. Across it, on either side of the road, you should see two small farms, each with a waist-high wall of stone. Scour the wall on the west side of the road for a stone unlike the rest. It is an almost perfect circle, its color the deep purple of a rich, Italian wine. Directly above that stone is the letter, sealed behind a plain, gray rock that the years have jarred loose from its mortar.

I realize this might be a tall order to fill. I realize that I stole this idea from one of my all-time favorite movies. And I also realize this scavenger hunt probably hasn't always been the easiest. Keep heart, though, and march on toward the end.

Everything will be worth it then.

And, if you really need a handicap, you can cheat with the GPS coordinates on the back of this page.

June 30, 2023

Dear Dad,

Sorry I haven't written you over the last couple days. There were a handful of occasions when I pulled journal and pen from my backpack, but for some reason I couldn't do it. My heart, and therefore my words, have felt so ... *blocked.* It's as if the business with Franco has clogged my emotional arteries so that nothing can flow through and out of me.

In your letter, you told me to keep a grasp on wonder. But wonder is dead. I know it isn't your fault. I shouldn't have pinned the blame on you for everything that happened in Alaska. Life just sucks right now, that's all. I was looking for an outlet, and you were the easiest target.

I had come to believe, even in such a short time, that Franco was the one for me. He made my heart sing a song I had never known before. Even after my many months with Andrew, I didn't truly see myself with him beyond the present.

Franco, on the other hand? I wanted him at my side a hundred years from now, and there wasn't a whisper of doubt about it.

That was what Andrew must have seen in me ... what I failed to see in him. Now I see it in Franco, but he cannot see it in me.

My, how the tables have turned.

I suppose everyone has to face these kinds of setbacks in life. Mom certainly has, and to far worse degrees than me, but her life isn't shrouded in despair. Neither will mine. I'll bounce back. I'll be whole again.

But at the moment, everything just plain sucks.

My flight to Denver leaves the day after tomorrow. I'll spend a couple weeks there until after Sam's wedding. Sam Gooding, that is. I'm sure you remember him! His parents are still pretty close with Mom. Anyway, I told Mom back in February that I'd go to the wedding, but I'm not exactly looking forward to it. The Murphy clan is bound to attend as well, and that means there's a good chance Andrew will be there with his medal-winning woman. (Sure puts a whole new spin on the phrase "trophy wife." Barf.) Plus, Mom has informed me that Gary is going. I mean, I'm happy for her, of course. It'll just be a lot of love thrown in my face all at once.

In the meantime, I'll distract myself planning the trip to Lucca. I've always wanted to go to Italy, even before you sent me zigzagging across the planet. Now I have an undeniable reason to pull the trigger, so I can at least thank you for that!

Not sure how much writing I'll do between now and then. I think I might need a short break from all these gushy feelings, and whenever I write to you lately, it's like I'm made of nothing *but* feelings.

Ugh. What have I become? This is your fault. Because of you, I'm a living, breathing, Nicholas Sparks tragedy.

Barf again!

Love, your (sad sap) little girl (who will hopefully quit being such a whiny little bitch soon),
Kate

July 16, 2023

Dear Dad,

My favorite history teacher in high school once told a story. It was about how the misunderstanding of a single word led to the deaths of hundreds of thousands of people. I've never researched it myself, so I can't say for sure if it's true or merely a fable, but apparently when the United States asked for Japan's surrender during World War II, the emperor responded in Japanese (as, I'm told, emperors from Japan are prone to do). He said something like "Wait for an answer, we're discussing it." The translation given to President Truman, however, was more along the lines of "F-off, a-hole." Truman then responded swiftly and severely by dropping a pair of atomic bombs on Hiroshima and Nagasaki.

Again, I can't be sure whether or not that actually happened, or if it's nothing more than a myth conflated by time. Regardless, I found out tonight that one of my own misunderstandings also led to disaster. Granted, the magnitude of my mistake's consequences can't begin to compare with what happened in Japan all those years ago, yet the result was disastrous in its own way.

Before I go on, we first have to back up a couple weeks. After returning home from Washington, I was still wallowing in the emotional refuse of my broken heart. I spent waaaaaay too much time in bed. And food? No thanks. Most of my waking life was spent motionless in front of old episodes of *The Office.* I tried to occupy myself with Italy plans, but I couldn't churn up the motivation to do much of anything.

Mom's the one who began hauling me up from my miry funk. After the fifth or sixth night of dealing with my pathetic moping, she strolled purposefully in front of my bedroom TV and switched it off.

"Sit up," she ordered. Her tone was sharper than anything I'd heard since the days when I was a whiny kid.

I almost didn't obey in time to catch the Coors she threw at my head.

"You know I don't like this crap," I mumbled. "Tastes like piss."

"Watch your mouth," she snapped, as she sat beside me and cracked a second can for herself. "Besides, if you're ever gonna make your dad proud, you better learn to like it."

Silently, I opened the beer, sucked the rising foam from the top of the can, and tried not to gag. At least it was freezing cold enough to temper my tastebuds.

"I know you don't like to talk much when something's bothering you," she said, "and usually I'm fine letting you deal with stuff your own way. But I've never seen you like this, Little Love. So you're gonna drink *that* Coors, and then this one"—my beer magician mother's hand suddenly held another can, which she thrust at me—"and once you're good and loosened up, you're gonna spill your guts about whatever happened in Alaska."

I opened my mouth to argue, but she didn't give me the chance as she stood and cut me off. "Be in the kitchen in ten minutes. The first two better be done by then, because there'll be a third waiting for you."

Ten minutes later, that's where I was. Lubricated by two cans of open-up juice, the story of me and Franco came pouring out of my mouth in all its tiny details, as if I were some kind of old-timey bard regaling the royal court with her epic tales. I've always been pretty tight-lipped about personal issues with Mom, especially the relationship stuff, but that evening I talked like I was trying to get my money's worth from a therapist.

When I had finished my woeful tale, Mom leaned back in her seat and said, "I told you Alaska would be dangerous. You didn't listen."

I rolled my eyes, chuckled, and replied, "Yeah, whatever. It wasn't *grizzlies,* Mom."

Ignoring my counterattack, she asked, "Now doesn't that feel better? Getting all that out?"

"Yeah, a bit," I answered meekly, unable to refrain from cracking a grin.

She shook her head with wistful amusement. "You and your dad ... always acting like you've got to shoulder every burden all on your own. For as little as you knew him, you're a lot like him. It's kinda scary, actually!"

The words from your Patagonia letter flooded back to mind. "That's funny," I said. "Dad wrote me and told me to make sure I'm somebody who accepts support from others. He said we aren't meant to carry life all on our own. Seems a little ... I don't know ... hypocritical?"

"Or maybe," Mom retorted, "he was humble enough to recognize his flaws and wanted better for you."

Gazing across the table at her, I expected to see the same veiled grief I'd witnessed when she spoke of you in the past, but this time she appeared calm, untroubled, at peace. Gary, it seems, is finally helping her move on. Now, I realize that's all I can do too. Even Andrew was able to push forward after our relationship ended.

And that segue, dear Dad, is how I cleverly transition you to the events of this evening and the realization of my great misunderstanding. Because, you see, it all involves Andrew and the events of this past winter.

Mom, Gary, and I arrived at Sam Gooding's wedding shortly before its two o'clock kickoff. Because most of the forward pews were already sagging beneath the butts parked in them, we selected a spot near the back of the aging country church. As I glanced around, I felt certain the three of us were the final arrivals, the kids who show up to class mere seconds before the bell rings. The only difference at a wedding is that you're stuck in the rear instead of within the teacher's spray radius.

It turns out we weren't the last to arrive. Moments before the triumphal procession commenced, a lone figure rushed into the sanctuary through a side door and planted himself next to me. He jumped like a snake-bit cowboy when he glanced over and realized he had chosen a seat at the hip of his ex-almost-fiancée.

"Howdy, Andrew," I whispered, offering him an awkward wave.

"H-hey, Kate," he stuttered. "I—uh—my parents are here, somewhere, but I got off work late and—"

The entrance of the first bridesmaid cut him short. Our uncomfortable encounter was mercifully muted by the procession, then the rest of the wedding. When the final bridal couple exited with their plastered-on grins, Andrew wasted no time standing up himself.

"I'll see you at the reception, I guess," he whispered.

I was about to tell him I looked forward to it, but he whirled about and left before I had the chance, melting into the afternoon heat through the same side door he had entered. Moments after his departure, I spotted his parents in the stop-and-go traffic crawling along the center aisle. There was, however, one glaring omission.

No Angela Martinez. Until then I had assumed she was sitting with Andrew's parents, waiting for her tardy boyfriend to join her. The truth was that she hadn't come to the wedding at all.

A flood of old desires broke unexpectedly through the levees of my heart. Almost reflexively, I discovered myself wondering whether Andrew and I might get another chance at things. Images of the romantic reception pulsed through my mind's eye like the scenes of a rom-com. Unable to help myself, I daydreamed of a dance. A reconciling conversation. A kiss.

As soon as I caught myself, I pushed the fantasy away. My smarter head reminded my dumbass heart that I had put the brakes on our relationship for a reason. Andrew was too domesticated, too safe. He was clingy and dramatic and incredibly codependent. Yet even as my head educated my heart, I found all my old arguments falling flat. I had grown up plenty in the last few months. Maybe he had too. Perhaps we had both learned enough about ourselves to rekindle our former flame.

Tonight, I thought, would be interesting.

The bride and groom held their reception at a local country club. For the hour before dinner, I did little more than split time between two activities: stealing glances at the front door for Andrew, and watching Mom and Gary googly-eyeing each other across the table.

When Andrew finally did enter, my stomach turned sour, and I heard my shattered fantasies raining down around me like the shards of a broken mirror.

Laced delicately between Andrew's fingers, were those of Angela Martinez. I hated how glamorous they appeared together (there was no way I ever looked that good next to him), but what I hated even more was the glittering engagement ring on her finger.

Mom noticed it too. Always the mind-reader, she put an arm around my shoulders and gave me a reassuring squeeze. I glanced back, offered a pathetic grin, and shrugged like it mattered no more to me than the Rockies losing one of their 162 games. Because ... well, what else *could* I do? We had both moved on. The only difference was that Andrew had moved on to a fiancée, and I had moved on to Franco's stinging rejection. I couldn't be mad at him, because I knew there was no one to blame but myself. Still, it needled me to watch them dancing after the dinner, talking close, beaming at each other, immersed in their fully ripened love.

The wine on my tongue only added fuel to the fires of my envy. Eventually, I could stand the spectacle no longer. "It's too hot in here," I told Mom, who was taking a break from dancing with Gary while he used the restroom. "I'm gonna cool off outside."

The first hole of the golf course kept me company for almost an hour as I strolled it up and down. For some reason, the darkness comforted me. It was like I could hide my inner turmoil from the whole world, including myself. My eyes wandered up toward the stars while I walked, and I couldn't help but wonder where Franco was at that moment and what he was doing. I don't know why, but thinking about him eased the pain I felt about Andrew's engagement, while at the same time reopening a different set of wounds.

There would be no winning for Kate, apparently, so I decided to leave the solitary darkness behind and rejoin the party. The moment I reached the front door, however, someone from inside threw it open and knocked me backward. Just as had happened at school back in May, that "someone" barging through the door was Andrew. This time there was no Angela with him. We were alone.

"Kate!" he exclaimed, grabbing my elbow to steady me. "Jeez, I'm sorry. I've gotta stop opening doors like the Hulk, or else I'm gonna kill someone sooner or later."

"It's OK," I replied, flustered. "Don't worry about it."

He stared at me for a moment, then asked, "Sooooo what are you doing out here anyway?"

I chuckled, scratched at the corner of my eye, and said, "I was taking a walk. Thinking."

Andrew said nothing. He stared, waiting for more of my story.

My typically stubborn self broke in an instant. "OK, I admit it, it's just a little hard to see you with her. And the engagement ring. Caught me off guard, I guess."

His expression softened. I read true remorse in his eyes as he replied, "Sorry if it feels like I'm throwing us in your face. We actually just got engaged yesterday. I suppose I should've realized I'd see you here at Sam's wedding, but I honestly didn't—"

"No." I cut him off. "No. You have nothing to explain, nothing to apologize for. It's just ... I dunno ... when you showed up to the wedding by yourself earlier, I started wondering if there might be a chance that ... Well, it doesn't matter, I guess."

Andrew kicked at a pebble on the cement and said, "She had swim practice this afternoon. That's why Ange wasn't at the ceremony."

An awkward silence followed. Unable to stand it any longer, and wanting nothing more than to escape, I muttered, "I'm glad you found someone to give that ring to, Andrew. I hope you'll be happy."

But there would be no escape for me. Not yet, anyway. Because Andrew raised an eyebrow and asked, "What do you mean, '*that* ring'?"

I stared at my toes, embarrassed. "That night in January, when I came back from Chile. I could tell you were going to propose, and I wasn't ready for it. That's why I panicked."

"Propose?" There was a bitterness in his laugh. "Kate, I wasn't going to propose that night. And there certainly wasn't any ring. I bought Angela's two weeks ago."

"But I saw you—thought I saw you, anyway—fiddling with something in your jacket pocket! And you were acting so nervous. *And* you were so insistent for us to go to that fancy restaurant."

"Sorry. I was a little out of sorts then. You'd been acting so distant," he explained. "I was worried you were gonna break up with me. I wanted to make some kind of grand, stupid gesture with the fancy restaurant. That's all. And I was right, by the way. About you breaking up with me."

"I just wanted to pump the brakes a little!" I exclaimed, a bit aggressively. "You kept talking so much about the future, and I wasn't ready." I cut myself off and took a deep breath.

Suddenly, and out of nowhere, a laugh escaped my lips. I gazed up into his kind face and said, "It doesn't matter anymore, does it. It's all in the past. For what it's worth, I'm sorry I jumped to that conclusion and made so many assumptions. I should have been more open. And honest. That's something I've been working on lately."

"It's OK, Kate," he replied. "Really. I let it go a long time ago."

"Yeah? Just like that?" I asked, skeptically and with an accompanying snap of my fingers. "After everything that happened, it was that easy?"

Andrew offered a passive shrug and answered, "I mean ... don't get me wrong, I was pretty mad at you for a while. But that day at school when we traded our stuff back to each other ... I guess I realized afterward that holding on to my anger wasn't helping. Not you, and certainly not me. So I decided to let it go. To forgive you, if there even was anything to forgive."

"Oh, there was," I squeaked, suddenly ashamed. "I was inconsiderate and impulsive and, well, *horrible.* But thank you. Thank you for telling me that. I needed to hear it. I've been pretty angry at myself recently for the way I treated you."

"Water under the bridge," he assured me. Then, eager to move the conversation toward an amicable conclusion, he added, "Besides, everything worked out, didn't it? I guess I should actually thank you. If you hadn't done that, I wouldn't have found my future wife. Everything happened the way it was supposed to."

"Yes," I agreed, though with my lips only. Not with my heart. "I'm really happy for you. And Angela."

"Thanks," he said, flashing me that million-dollar grin. "Well, I better go get the car. I told Ange I'd pull it up so she wouldn't have to walk to the back of the parking lot. Sore feet. Heels. You know how it is."

"Yeah. Sure. Bye, Andrew."

"See ya, Kate."

With that, Andrew disappeared into the darkness, and I returned to the warm lighting of the reception hall. The night went on. The party ended. We went home.

Now here I am, alone because of a stupid misunderstanding back in January. I didn't have all the information, and it ended in the fiery wreckage of my relationship with Andrew. But perhaps that misunderstanding only sped along a breakup that was inevitable anyway. I'd always had my doubts about Andrew being "the one." In the end, my assumptions might have saved a lot of time—both for me *and* for Andrew.

But there's something else. Something keeping me up. Something which has led to me writing this long, drawn-out story late into the night.

Maybe my misunderstanding with Andrew wasn't the only one that ended in disaster. What if, in Alaska, some version of the same thing happened again with Franco? Was there some missing information, some hidden slice of either his life or mine, which in mere moments turned his eager kiss into that swift dismissal? I suppose I might never have satisfactory answers to those questions. There's a good chance I'll never even see Franco again. But tonight I learned something from my conversation with Andrew. If I want clear answers, if I want the whole story, I can't live beneath the shadows of my assumptions. That road leads only to disaster.

I have to ask. I have to open myself up to the possibility of even deeper rejection. I have to swallow my ego, and my pride, and my stubbornness by laying bare my innermost self to Franco and praying he'll do the same for me.

I may not know where he is, but I do have a phone number and an email address. Tomorrow I will hold my bleeding heart out before him. I will let him choose whether to take it as his own or refuse it.

That's all I can do. That's all I have left. Whatever happens afterward, I'll be proud of myself for taking the leap.

And, somehow, I know you'll be proud of me too.

Love, your (done-with-assumptions) little girl,
Kate

July 18, 2023

Dear Dad,

It's been two days. No answer from Franco.

I guess that's what you get sometimes. I sent him a long email. I tried calling him twice. Yesterday I even left a voicemail, asking him to call me back.

Nothing. Maybe he's still enjoying his Alaskan adventure. Maybe he's in the middle of nowhere, miles away from cell service.

Or maybe he wants nothing more to do with me. I still don't understand why, but maybe we aren't meant to understand everything that happens in this life.

Whatever the case, I'm done sitting around the house moping. Sure, it sucks ass, but I can't let it defeat me. I'm gonna walk away from this, grab life by the balls, and soak up as much as I can.

Tomorrow I leave for Italy. I'm picking up the adventure you gave me, the one I almost abandoned in Alaska. I would like to think, even in the last few weeks, that I've learned something new.

I've learned that I cannot attach my heart, my life, to a person. To do so is to give up all power over my happiness. I will instead hold on to these things myself. Then, as long as I have me, I will also have joy and purpose and wonder. And if someone, someday, comes along with whom I can share myself completely, the joy of self I already possess will only increase all the more.

Maybe that's what you meant when you told me no one is truly independent. We don't *need* other people to be fulfilled and content. We can know and experience that self-satisfaction on our own. We are fully capable of basking in the light of our own lives' radiance. Yet at the same time, we should never reject an opportunity to find company among the other brilliant stars surrounding us in our universe. Somehow, in this paradoxical way, a person's interdependence upon others works hand-in-hand with autonomy and self-sufficiency.

That, I believe, may be life's recipe for a truly beautiful dance.

Love, your (pondering) little girl,
Kate

July 21, 2023

Dear Dad,

Holy frickin' crap, this place is cool! The area, the city, the hostel, *everything.* (Other than my being tired as hell, that is.)

A rash of severe weather stretching from London to Berlin turned my overnight connection to Florence into a full day of unexpected layover in Paris. Instead of lazing about the airport, bitching about the cancellations like everyone else, I immersed myself as deeply as I could in the City of Lights. It was evening by the time I was finished visiting the Eiffel Tower, Arc de Triomphe, and Notre Dame Cathedral. Once back at Charles de Gaulle, I slept (if you can actually call it sleep) on a quiet corner of airport floor and woke up to catch my early-morning flight to the birthplace of the Italian Renaissance.

After the plane was safely aground in Florence, I hopped a westbound train through the rolling fields and villages of Tuscany. It deposited me here, at this ancient city from a fairy tale, encircled completely by a wall so broad, people have driven cars on top of it! I read that there's a walking path wrapping all the way around Lucca, complete with plenty of benches to sit and stare at the golden landscape in silence.

Once inside the city gates, I navigated myself along the narrow cobblestone streets toward my hostel. The ancient dwellings of Lucca constrict these winding roadways, creating a looming sense of claustrophobia. I guess I'm not used to feeling like a sardine.

After getting myself lost a dozen different times, I managed to locate the hostel. The clerk who showed me to my private room explained how it was built four hundred years ago and used to be a convent. He also shared rumors about it being haunted, but assured me most of the spirits here are friendly ones who protect the hostel's inhabitants (though it does make a girl wonder what the few *un*friendly ones might do to visitors).

Since the next location you gave me is a ways outside of town, I'm going to wait until tomorrow to search for your letter. If it hasn't gone anywhere after all this time, I don't think one more night will make a difference. In the interim, I'm gonna score myself a genuine Italian pizza, select a bottle of Tuscany's finest local wine, and park my ass somewhere on top of the city wall. There, I will watch the sun sink down below the golden hills.

I can't think of anything better.

Love, your (reborn) little girl,
Kate

July 22, 2023

Dear Dad,

Where do I begin telling the story that's unfolded over the past day? From the moment I ended my previous letter? From the inaugural bite of gooey, cheesy wondrousness known as Italian pizza? From the first drop of intoxicating wine that hit my lips? From the surprise that lifted me higher than the Renaissance walls of this town ever could? Or from the defeat that buried me lower than their foundations?

How about I start on the downer note, then backpedal to the uplifting one?

I'm sorry, Dad, but I didn't find your letter today. I never will. It's gone. I must have followed that road, the Via per Camaiore, for three miles before I realized your landmark was no longer there. Even early on, I could sense something wasn't right. When you hid your letter, the area north of town must have been rural territory, dotted with quaint, Tuscan farmsteads and their stone fences like those I saw from the train. Now, twenty years later, the miles north of town have become much more developed. Modern Italy, it seems, has no more use for ancient boundary fences.

To double check, I made use of a GPS app on my phone. (I know you gave me your GPS to use, but you need to get with the times, Dad. We use phones for *literally* everything in 2023.) Sure enough, where your entombed letter once waited, there now stands a gas station with convenience store, a metal-and-concrete monument to the supremacy of the present and the death of the past. Undoubtedly some crude piece of construction machinery snatched away your letter and carried it to a dump far away from here.

My father's legendary legacy, destroyed by humanity's corporate needs.

Truth be told, I'm surprised I made it this far. It was only a matter of time before my luck ran off, carrying one of your letters in hand. I admit that I had become hopeful. With only a couple left I thought I might beat the odds. I hope you didn't have, like, buried treasure waiting for me at the end. Because the chain is broken. The game is up. The journey is over.

Or maybe, in another sense, it has only just begun. If you let me rewind to yesterday, I can explain what I mean.

After I finished writing my letter to you, I did exactly as planned. At a tiny table set upon the cobblestone courtyard outside a café, I gorged myself on pizza. Then I bought a fancy bottle of rich, purple *vino* from a wine depot across the plaza. On top of the Great Wall of Lucca, I found a westward-facing bench sheltered beneath the rustling leaves of a poplar tree. I watched, breathless, as the retiring sun turned the backdrop of rolling hills into a masterpiece of molten bronze and fiery amber and deep gold.

That was when a voice behind me spoke my name.

Sick elation seized my heart, as if a hand were grabbing and squeezing it. I stood, turned, saw him.

Franco. In the flesh. In Lucca. Constantly cool and confident, he was more nervous than I had ever seen him.

"What—*how?* What are you doing here? How did you ...?"

"Your mother told me you were coming here," Franco explained. He stepped awkwardly forward until within reach of me.

And yet he did not reach for me.

"But how did you find *her?*" I demanded.

"Her number was in my phone," he said. "Remember? You used it to call her at the Denali visitor center. When I saw your email, when I heard your message, I knew I had to find you. I had to tell you ..."

"Tell me what?" I asked when he trailed off. Part of me was ecstatic to see him. Another part was guarded and untrusting.

He sighed and said, "Everything."

"Then ... come, sit with me," I replied, and parked myself again on the bench. "Watch the sun."

Franco did. Sweet aromas of fresh soap and newly laundered clothes greeted me. He had obviously taken the time to spruce himself up before his quest to find me. Yet it was the earthy scent of Franco himself, buried beneath the artificial ones, that set me at ease. It instilled in me a warm sort of comfort, like curling up beneath a pile of cozy blankets on a drizzly autumn afternoon.

"So? What do you need to tell me?" I asked after a half minute of his hesitation. If he wanted to stall or back down, I wasn't going to let him.

"I ... I have a daughter, Kate."

That strangled sensation around my heart tightened. If Franco had been wondering what revelation might shock me more than his sudden presence in Lucca, he'd found a winner. Still, I said nothing. He clearly had more to share.

"I was married once," he went on, "though not for long. We were only nineteen, Elena and I. We knew each other and loved each other since we were twelve years old. Even when I spent my exchange year in California, we continued together, sending long emails and video-chatting as often as we could. We were going to spend our lives together. That's why it made sense to get married after high school."

Franco paused. He was willing himself the courage to proceed with his confession. For a few seconds he stared into the indigo sky above the distant Tuscan hills. Then he turned his gaze at me. This seemed to supply the strength he needed to go on, so he said, "We were so poor, Kate. I wanted to give her a better life. That's why I became involved in ... some illegal activities. One of my childhood friends had an uncle involved in the cocaine business, so I went to work for him."

I grabbed his arm firmly, interrupting his story. The pain in his eyes was as real as if he'd been stabbed.

"You don't need to go on with this. Anything you don't want to tell me, you don't have to, Franco."

But he shook his head and replied, "No. I need you to know who I am."

"OK," I sighed. I wasn't sure I wanted to hear more.

"Elena always thought I was working extra shifts at my construction job," Franco continued. "I was working there, yes. But for a few hours in the late afternoon I was working my other job, too. The whole time, I told myself that I would never personally use what I was selling. I would reap all the benefits and none of the destruction. But soon, I found out how hard it is to be part of something without sinking deeper into it. Before I knew what I was doing, I had started using. I convinced myself it would just happen here and there, little bits to relieve the stress that comes with working an illegal enterprise. Of course, that is not how such things work. My usage grew and grew. Elena knew something was different about me, but she didn't know what. At least, not for a while.

"Then she became pregnant. When she told me, I promised myself I was done with the drugs. For three weeks I managed to stay clean. But the hooks were already set too deep inside me, and I fell back into it. The new pressures of fatherhood, of knowing I would soon have another mouth to feed and care for ... it was so much weight on me. One night I came home, wasted far beyond anything ever before. That is when Elena knew for certain. We fought, first with only our words. But then I ..."

Franco's voice failed him, swept away by the flood of tears now cascading down his cheeks. He buried his head in his hands, composed himself, wiped his eyes dry, and went on.

"Then I started fighting with my hands. I hit her. Hard. Just once, but it was enough. Immediately I came to myself, but the damage was done. Irreversible. I begged her forgiveness. She begged me to leave. She said if I didn't, she would call the police. That was her mercy for me. I stayed out of prison in exchange for staying out of her life."

"Franco ..."

"I have never seen my daughter," he said, ignoring me. "My Maria. Elena has sent me a few pictures and videos over the years, out of pity more than anything, but I have never heard her laugh with my own ears. I have never kissed her round, beautiful face. I have never held her hand while crossing the street. She is seven years old now. Elena remarried a few months ago, so my daughter has a new papa named Ronaldo. He has adopted her. And even though so much time has passed, even though I have never seen her with my own two eyes, I love her more than anything."

Franco choked up again. This time, he didn't try to collect himself before saying, "I'll never be her father, her protector, because she must stay protected from me. And that is a pain I cannot bear. It is a pain I have run from for the last seven years. That is why I became a park ranger far, far away from my hometown. I had loved my family's vacation to the Torres so much as a child. I wanted to protect *something* I loved. Maybe then I could forget the damage I caused. I desired so badly to escape the shadow of the life I had lost. The life I destroyed."

Staring directly into me, he said, "It is why, when you kissed me, I pushed you away. I have never been able to protect the people I love. They have always needed protection from me! So how can I be for you, Kate, what I failed to be for all the others? That is the answer to the question you asked me in the hospital. That is the reason I cannot be with you. Do you understand?" When finished, he buried his face in his hands.

For a moment, I gazed out at the plum-tinted hills below the darkening sky. I'd always figured Franco had something unpleasant to hide. As long as I'd known him, he'd been guarded about his past. I did not, however, expect anything quite like this. My stomach sickened. Revulsion began crawling up my throat.

Then, just as quickly, it fell away. The memory of a conversation, not even a full week old, spread from conscious thought to my heart. My breast and throat and cheeks flushed with a familiar warmth.

Andrew's words of forgiveness had calmed the raging voice of guilt inside me. Although I had not been the victim of Franco's confessed transgressions, I now had the duty to give him something of what Andrew had given me.

"Franco," I spoke tenderly, prying his fingers from his face to hold it in my own, "what you told me wasn't completely true. A minute ago, you said you needed me to know who you are. But that man you described—he isn't who you *are*. He's who you *were*. There's a difference."

Still, he would not meet my gaze. Like words on a page, I read shame and self-loathing in his face.

Since he wouldn't speak, I went on and said, "You did something bad. *Really* bad."

He cocked his head and furrowed his brow, as if silently saying, *No shit, Nancy Drew.*

"But we've all done bad things," I went on, wiping away one of his tears with my thumb. "Look, I'm not saying Elena will ever forgive you, or even that she should. But maybe instead of everyone sitting around, pointing fingers, grading others as worse people than themselves—like there's some kind of cosmic moral curve they'll get to the front of—what we really need from each other is understanding. And compassion. And *forgiveness.* Because we all need another chance."

"You would give me this?" Franco was blinking away tears, staring at me with hopeful disbelief.

"Somebody has to!" I exclaimed with a grin. "And I want to be your somebody."

With that, I pulled him in for a kiss. This time he did not pull away. I don't know how long it went on. For all I know, time might have stopped in that Tuscan paradise. Eventually, though, our lips did break apart. As I stared into those chocolatey Chilean eyes only inches from mine, I said, "But if you ever think about hurting me, I promise, I will kill you. Understand?"

"You already tried once in Alaska," he replied. "I have no doubts you could do it again."

Like a kid whose hand is in the cookie jar when mom rounds the corner, my eyes shot open. Now it was my turn for a slice of shame-and-embarrassment pie.

Franco chuckled and said, "Yes, I know about the aspirin. I overheard the nurses in the hospital making jokes about you."

"I'm *so* sorry," were the only words I could find. I fumbled to gather a few more, but Franco held up a hand to stop me.

"Let's assume we have both learned from our mistakes," he reassured me, his tone that of a man making a solemn oath. "I will only ever love you, Kate."

"Good." I kissed him again. "And don't worry, I already threw the rest of the aspirin away. Don't think I'll be able to look at another bottle for the rest of my life."

There was another kiss, longer, deeper, fuller than any before it. I hoped it would never end, but I guess everyone has to come up for air sometime. Once we finally had, Franco brushed a strand of blond hair from my forehead and asked, "So, where do you go next?"

I shrugged and replied, "I don't know. I haven't gone to find Dad's letter yet. Based on what I read in Washington, though, I do know there's only one more stop after Lucca."

He pressed my hand between his own, kissed me, and said, "You must finish this on your own. I cannot come with you."

I raised an eyebrow. "Why not? I mean, you came all this way ..."

"Like I said at the Torres, this is between a father and his daughter. As for me, I have my own father-daughter issue to take care of back home. You gave me a second chance. Maybe Elena will give me a second chance to become a father to my little girl." He must have noticed the flash of concern my expression betrayed, because he added, "I promise you, I will be with you when this is over. For good. Elena is my past. You are my present, and you are my future."

My heart became filled with wonder as I whispered, "Can't wait, Franco."

He left me this morning. Right now he's traveling to his hometown, praying that Elena will give him another chance. Not the chance that the two of them will get back together, but another chance to see his daughter and to be her dad. I hope she gives him that opportunity. Whether she does or doesn't, he has promised to visit me once my own journey is over.

And that journey's end appears to be right now. I'll enjoy another evening here, letterless, with another pizza and another bottle of wine, watching another sunset from Lucca's sturdy walls. It'll be the celebration of my defeat, I guess. Then, in the morning, I will pack my bags and return to Colorado.

Maybe someone else will stumble across your buried treasure someday. When they do, I hope they'll find in your letter a degree of the warmth and joy that I found in them.

Damn. This really does suck. But there ain't much I can do about it now, except graciously accept my defeat.

I better fire off a quick message to Mom. She'll want to know I'm heading home tomorrow.

Then ... pizza and wine! (At least your letters led me to those treasures!)

Love, your (soundly defeated) little girl,
Kate

July 23, 2023

Dear Dad,

My heart aches to leave this wonderful place. Yet here on the plane, after reflecting on my journeys, I realize I have to give you a compliment. You really did choose places I'll love and remember for the rest of my life, even if I never return to them. It's almost as if you knew exactly who I would become and handpicked the places you were sure would resonate with me.

I do wish I could have seen the end of the trail you blazed for me, though now I realize it would have only been a milestone and not the finish line. You see, you've planted the seeds of adventure deep down inside me. Even if this leg of our journey together is over, I'll continue doing what you did. I'll carry on your legacy. Yes, I may be back in Colorado tomorrow, but now I know I can make this big wide world my home.

And don't worry. I have a few pages left over to keep writing about those adventures! (You didn't think you were getting away from me *that* easily, did you?) Until then, know that wherever I am, I love you. Even though I'm sure you have a bajillion mind-blowing things to do up there, I hope you'll still take some time out of eternity to watch over your Cuddles.

She finally realizes just how much she needs you.

Love, your (forever grateful) little girl,
Kate

---------- SEVEN ----------

The Best Laid Plans

July 24, 2023

Dear Dad,

I bet you think you're one clever S.O.B., don't you! Mom told me you were the kind of person who prided himself on his annoyingly thorough plans. I'm happy to let you know that, yet again, your foresight and preemptive troubleshooting have saved the day.

I arrived around seven in the morning at JFK International in New York City, emotionally and physically exhausted from a series of connecting flights and minor delays. Now back in the good ol' US-of-A, I turned on my cell service for the first time in over a day. Before any notifications could come through, I texted Mom to let her know my flight to Denver would be on time. No sooner had I hit the *SEND* button than my phone *dinged* with a message. Turns out I had an email from Mom waiting in my inbox. The subject line read: *URGENT! BEFORE YOU LEAVE ITALY!*

Just a little late for that, Mom ...

You already know what she revealed. Hell, I should have known it too. In your very first letter at Christmas, you straight up told me to check in with Mom if I hit a roadblock. Apparently you had a crazy hunch that human development might pave over one or more of your poor letters. That's why you came up with a Plan B. Before you died, you left in her care backup copies of every letter you wrote me. At the end of her email explaining all this, she attached a handful of images containing your second-to-last letter.

I didn't look at them. It would've felt wrong for some reason, reading your letters on a screen. So I came up with a different idea instead.

Currently, Mom is preparing for her own trip. Tomorrow morning, she'll fly out of Denver to join me here in New York. The moment she hands it to me, I will read your letter. I'll learn the location of your scavenger hunt's grand finale. Then Mom and I will travel there ... *together.* Yes, she insisted at the start of all this that I go solo, but when I found out you had entrusted all those backup letters to her, an instant epiphany bit me square on the ass. From the very first day, Mom has been an invested party in this game of yours. Maybe, in some ways, even more so than myself. It must've been killing her to sit on the sidelines, hearing only my vague, infrequent reports about where I'd gone and what I'd been up to. Before they were my adventures, they'd been *her* adventures with you. Leaving herself out of this, your final global game, must have been a strange and lonely sort of torture.

Well, not anymore! She hasn't run the whole race with me, but she will be by my side at the finish line.

Both of your girls ... and you, Dad. You couldn't have bargained for anything better.

Can't wait to read your Lucca letter when Mom gets here!

Love, your (renewed) little girl,
Kate

June 17th, 2003

(If you're reading this version of the letter, it means my plans in Lucca fell on their face. That's life, I suppose! As I've already said, our plans don't always pan out the way we envision them, and here's Exhibit A. So, thank God for backup plans! Right now, you're holding mine. Everything below this is an exact copy of my original letter to you.)

Dear Kate—

When most people hear the word *alchemy*, images of eccentric, ancient Greeks transforming lead into gold fill their minds. Certainly this was one goal of the early alchemists, the transmutation of common metals into more valuable ones. The irony of the pursuit, of course, was that if someone had actually succeeded, the rarer metals would suddenly lose their value by becoming common themselves. Kings and other rulers understood how this might cheapen their own vast stores of wealth, which is why many outlawed the practice of alchemy in their dominions. After a time, the Greek alchemists abandoned their quest altogether.

What few people know is that alchemy made a brief resurgence among these gilded hills of Tuscany during the Italian Renaissance. The pursuit of these academics was not so much aimed at the transmutation of base metals into precious ones, but of mortality into everlasting life. Whereas many recognized the irony in an ability to create unlimited gold, I'm not sure anyone saw the similar irony in trying to create unlimited time. If someone had succeeded in discovering the fabled Elixir of Life, time itself would have lost its value. No longer scarce and limited for each person, our moments would become cheap, unappreciated, *common.*

After all, isn't that the way younger people actually do view their time? When we are in our teens and twenties, we act as if time is unlimited. Our moments will never end. We are certain there will always be another tomorrow. What results is one of the saddest truths I've come to learn about humanity: We treat time cheaply. We view the seconds of our lives the way a multibillionaire must look at one-dollar bills, like they're nothing.

When I consider how much of my own life I lived that way, it sickens me. It is, perhaps, what I hate most about my past.

Oddly enough, my terminal diagnosis wasn't the catalyst that finally changed my perspective on time. As already mentioned, I was stubbornly committed to beating my sickness. Once I did, time would be unlimited again.

The change occurred on your ninth monthday. It was the day I thought I killed you.

Everything happened so fast. I was holding you in the kitchen. You were drinking milk out of your sippy cup. Without warning, you decided to spike your cup at the floor. I tried to catch it with one hand. You squirmed, leaned back, slipped from the grasp of my other arm.

Your head hit the hardwood first. The *crack!* of contact between your skull and the ground still haunts my nightmares. You lay there, perfectly still, for a skipped heartbeat's moment in time.

I was sure you were dead.

Then you started crying, sat up, reached for me. You were miraculously alright. Scared but unhurt, other than a tiny bump and bruise.

That event triggered a realization within me, and I've never been able to shake it.

Time is one fickle bitch.

Feels a little weird writing that to an eighteen-month-old. But it's true. (Plus, I keep reminding myself you'll be a young woman by the time you actually read my letters.)

Time doesn't care how long you've lived, or whether you're aware that it's about to run dry. Lucky people, like myself, receive some warning. Others it cuts short in the prime of life—car accidents, gun violence, heart attacks, falling pianos and anvils—without so much as a courtesy call. We people go most of our lives spending time like there's an infinite supply. Only when we realize we're running out do we clamor for more of it. And yet, try as we might, we cannot store up more for ourselves than what Time has allotted to us. There is no Elixir of Life to provide a little extra. In an instant, it is gone.

Time is fickle. Unpredictable, yet unyielding.

The only decision Time places in our hands is this: "What will I do with the amount allotted to me?"

Good God, Kate, *make the most of it.* I often think about my younger days now, how I wasted hour after hour catatonic in front of the TV like some sort of zombie who fed on blue light and MTV. *Every* second is one you will never get back. Remember that. Recognize that before you waste any more of it.

If there were a reason for me *not* to wait until your twenty-first birthday to send you on this scavenger hunt, that would be it. Twenty-one years are too many to waste, to spend in the drudgery of idle afternoons, or working jobs you hate, or with boyfriends who suck, or whatever else you look back upon and regret as time cheaply spent.

Kate, you only own a certain number of ticks on the clock. You have no idea how many belong to you. They might end tomorrow. So don't waste any more. Not a second. Not a millisecond. Discover whatever it is that will fill each moment with meaning, and spend your every breath doing exactly that.

If I had known this, I would have had you in my life a hell of a lot earlier. Then I might have enjoyed three more years with you, or three more months, or three more days. Even three more seconds of my Cuddles would have been three less wasted.

I want those three seconds back. But I won't get them. I spent them on something else. Something far less worth my time. Here, at the end, I regret it deeply.

But it's not the end for you. If you're reading this, it means you still have time. There isn't one thing you can change about the past, so don't waste precious moments trying. Focus on what you have. Focus on what is coming. Make those valuable seconds—*all* those seconds—as meaningful as possible.

That is how you well spend your most precious commodity.

I love you now and always,
Dad

With that, we're down to the last letter. In order to find it, you will now have to travel to the Látrabjarg bird cliffs, my runner-up for title of "Dad's Favorite Place on Earth." This final journey will require an investment of time and patience unlike any before it.

First, you must book a flight to Reykjavik, Iceland. Rent a car and drive north toward the region known as the Westfjords. Many hours of dirt roads, high passes, and otherworldly vistas later, if you have gone as far northwest as you can, you will find yourself at the bird cliffs. Enjoy here a walk along the edge of the European continental shelf. Never in my life have I found such a haven of tranquility as this—as long as the weather isn't too wild, that is! Thousands—millions—of seabirds have found refuge and safety upon these cliffs, where they build their nests a quarter mile above the thundering sea.

Your job is to find the highest of these cliffs. From its pinnacle, using my compass, head due north. Don't be turned from your path by anything—not a rock, not a hole, not wind, not rain. Nothing. If you follow the needle north, you'll find a mound of eight rocks. Move them out of the way and dig. This is where you will find it.

The final envelope. My last legacy to you.

Unlike before, I have no GPS coordinates to help you along. Nor are there any backup copies kept safe by your mom. If you don't find it, no one will be able to help you. My final gift will be lost forever.

This is the way it has to be. You may not understand now, but you will when you see it.

Search hard, Kate. I have no reason to think mankind would ever accidentally stumble upon this. So if it takes a day, or three, or a week, or even a month, I hope you won't give up.

Because my beating heart itself awaits you there.

Not literally.

July 26, 2023

Dear Dad,

Mom and I spent a full day together enjoying the gaudy lights and colorful sounds of the Big Apple. In the morning, we strolled through gardens in Central Park and stacks of books in the New York Public Library. The afternoon was filled with a food tour and getting lost on the subways.

So far, I think our daughter-mother trip is off to a great start!

During one of those underground train expeditions, Mom did grow pensive and quiet at one moment. When I asked her what was wrong, she said, "Nothing. It's just ... I haven't been out of the country since your dad died. I never went anywhere before I met him, either. My entire life beyond America's borders, your dad was always there. It'll be weird, you know? Going without him."

I reacted the only way I could. I wrapped my arms around her, laid my head on her shoulder, and said absolutely nothing. Sometimes the best response is nothing but a hug paired with utter silence.

Now we're back at the airport. Our flight to Iceland leaves soon, and I just wanted to take a hot second to let you know we're on our way.

I don't think you'll blame me for keeping this short. Somehow, I'm pretty sure you would approve of me focusing my time (precious as you say it is!) on the person sitting next to me instead of burying my head in this journal.

Mom says "Hi," by the way. Maybe this whole Gary thing is good for her. She didn't even get misty-eyed when we started talking about you!

Sorry if that stings, but it *has* been twenty long-ass years. About time for her to get over you!

She's mad at me for writing "ass" in the journal. Says I should rip this page out and start over.

I told her "Hell no." Now I'm in even more trouble. Better go!

Love, your (Iceland-bound) little girl,
Kate

July 27, 2023

Dear Dad,

My first day in Iceland left a rather rotten taste in my mouth. Literally. Mom and I went out for lunch when we arrived in the quaint, colorful city of Reykjavik. Our waiter convinced me I should try an Icelandic delicacy, *hákarl*, on his dime. It was probably well worth the laugh he enjoyed when I smelled it. When I actually tasted that shit, he almost died in hysterics. That's when he told me that *hákarl* is essentially rotten, fermented shark. It isn't customary for people to tip waiters here, so I guess he figured the prank would cost him nothing.

Tomorrow we're picking up our rental car, but we won't be making a beeline for the bird cliffs. Now that I have Mom with me, I want to soak up this time with her. So we're first gonna drive around the southern parts of the island. We want to see a few of Iceland's epic waterfalls, geysers, and black sand beaches. We'll visit glaciers, ancient churches, and the site of the world's first parliament gatherings.

In short, we'll go where we feel like going, and we'll do what we feel like doing. No more running around following only your agenda! It'll be a *real* vacation.

But before we embark on our great Icelandic expedition, I thought I would fill you in on the most recent email from Franco. I'm sure you've grown pretty invested in his story, so I'm also sure you've been tossing and turning at night, wondering how that loose thread might be unraveling. After all, you *have* been the third wheel since the beginning of our relationship!

Anyway, Franco told me that his mother (whom his ex-wife has allowed to be part of her granddaughter's life) convinced Elena to let Franco meet their little girl. Her new husband protested pretty adamantly against the reunion. In the end, Franco was allowed to see her, but he had to agree that he would introduce himself as a "friend" of her mom, and not as her father.

If real life were like a movie, he could have walked away from the meeting finally feeling whole again, the missing piece of his heart's puzzle locked into place at long last. Sadly, that's not how real life goes. He was definitely glad to see her with his own two eyes, hug her and feel her with his own hands. Now, though, he says there is a fresh sadness, because the most he can ever be, in his daughter's eyes, is a random friend of the family.

"I have to love her the best way I can," he wrote to me, "and I know what this means. It means I must leave them alone. Believe me, I wish it did not have to be this way, but it is where my choices have led. Maria is such a beautiful, content, funny little girl. And I cannot disrupt that. I cannot throw her life and her stability into disarray for my own selfish desire to be part of it. I must live as best I can beneath the consequences of my choices, even if I made them long ago. I will not bring fresh troubles upon Maria by making another selfish choice."

When I read that ... damn, I sure wish I could be there for him. It's a lot for one person to carry alone. His tone over email sounded confident and at peace with the decision, but I wonder how he's handling the disappointment when he can't hide behind a screen.

The email did end with a note of hope. It's one I need you to hear, Dad.

Franco wrote: "I keep thinking about your father. He was dealt a losing hand by no choice of his own, but he played the cards he was given. He made the most of it. When so many would have lived out their days in self-pity and despair, he made sure his time mattered to the people he loved the most. And that is what I must do for Elena and Maria. I will take care of them however I can, even if it must be from a distance. Just this morning I started a university fund for Maria, and I am committed to sending them money each month. Maria may never know who I really am, but I will know she is fed and cared for and has an education. This is how I will love her. This is how I will now make the most of my time as her father."

I know you never planned this, Dad, but in some crazy way I think you also helped save the man I love. Your life didn't only make an impact while you had a heartbeat. The way you chose to spend your time continues reaching further and deeper, even when you are two decades into your grave.

That's what I call making the most of a life.

Love, your (very-proud-of-her-daddy) little girl,
Kate

August 3, 2023

Dear Dad,

Our touring around Iceland has been nothing short of extraordinary. Never in my life have the bonds between me and Mom been stronger than this trip has forged them. Over the last week, I've seen sides of her I never knew existed. She's adventurous and carefree out here, willing to take each day as it comes to her. Perhaps this is who she always has been, but her duties as mother and provider held these qualities at bay. I'm older now, and this trip together may be proving to her that those roles, while necessary for my upbringing, can finally change. Whatever the case, this has been one of the best weeks of my entire life.

But our laidback days of traipsing wantonly about Iceland have come to their end. Last night, we stayed in a cozy cabin somewhere in the north-central-west-ish part of the island, and this morning we blazed our trail across the Westfjords. Like an infinite rope unwinding along the seacoast, the rugged road led us into and through another of Iceland's brilliant fantasy landscapes. What I can't figure out is why a bajillion bajillionaires haven't built their own private getaways in this quiet, breathtaking corner of the world. Every twist and turn of the road delivers a vista more astonishing than the one before it. If Mom weren't constantly nagging me to keep my eyes on the road, I for sure would have driven over a cliff and into a fjord.

I guess I could think of worse ways to die.

In the early evening's pale light we drove past a white sand beach. It was the only one we've encountered so far on this entire island. For some reason, it gave me hope. If that beach can exist here year after year, a unicorn among all the black, volcanic sands surrounding this island, then maybe your letter has somehow survived all this time as well. I know it's a bit stupid or illogical to compare the two, but I guess I've changed a lot on this journey. I'm starting to realize that living a totally logical life is a touch overrated.

Since it was getting late, we stopped for the night at a little hotel just shy of the bird cliffs. We'll want to be well-rested tomorrow, in case we have to search the whole day for your rock pile and the letter—your *last* letter—waiting beneath it.

It's strange to think that's where this long journey will an end. My head and my heart are working on overdrive as I wonder and wonder what final treasure of words you've left there for me. After the life-changing journey we've already had together, I have no idea what ultimate trick you might be hiding up your sleeve!

Let's hope there's enough magic left to pull this off.

Love, your (intrepid) little girl,
Kate

August 4, 2023

Dear Dad,

I can see why those cliffs rank among your top two places on all of planet Earth. What could possibly overtake this for that #1 spot?! I don't know that I've ever felt so at peace as I did at Látrabjarg, as the calls of the myriad seabirds rang out across the breeze, and the well-traveled swells of the North Atlantic crashed against the cliff's foundation far below. (At one point a curious puffin landed so close to us, I could have reached out and touched it!)

Those cliffs swelled me with such serenity, in fact, that I hardly cared about the day's great failure. I couldn't find your letter, Dad. Part of the problem, I'll admit, was that I stupidly forgot your compass at the hotel and was too stubborn to go back for it.

I'm sure tomorrow will be a different story. (And, I hope, the conclusion of yours!)

Love, your (determined) little girl,
Kate

August 6, 2023

Dear Dad,

Mom told me a parable today. I don't remember the exact details, but it was about an old copper miner who lived long ago. The story went that he sold all his possessions, his house, and his land back East so he could buy and mine copper-rich land out in Utah. His big dreams of striking it rich, however, quickly butted heads with reality. Every time he thought he'd found the mother lode of copper, he would bring it up to the surface. But whenever he inspected his haul in the daylight, he realized it wasn't the hard, bronze mineral he was seeking. Instead, he kept pulling out some kind of softer, yellow mineral. It seemed useless, so he would dump it into a big pile a good distance away from his mineshaft and resume digging.

He never found the copper he was looking for. After years and years of failure, and with only a gigantic pile of the worthless yellow rock to show for his labors, he was ruined. He took to drinking night after night. Finally, one evening, seething in a stew of booze and depression, the old miner shot and killed himself.

The local deputy read the poor man's tale in his autobiographical suicide note. But when the deputy investigated and found the pile of "worthless" mineral, his jaw dropped. The old miner had been so fixated on finding one specific treasure, he never realized he'd discovered a far more valuable one! For there, in the poor man's garbage heap, were tons and tons of solid gold.

Mom's reason for telling the story was plain. The last three days, I've been obsessively searching for your final letter. I've come away empty-handed every time.

But as I look back on the past months since Christmas, I have to wonder: Perhaps I already have the real treasure.

A story of my own. A story I can be proud of.

When you sent me off on this journey, you called it a scavenger hunt. I don't know why, but today I remembered back to how I explained the idea of a "scavenger hunt" to Franco. I told him it's when you either have clues that lead you to something, or when you find a bunch of random things to take home with you. Undoubtedly, your intention in fashioning this scavenger hunt was to lead me somewhere. By following your clues, I'd arrive at the *X* on your treasure map. I wonder, though, if the unintended consequence was actually the latter. You sent me off on a scavenger hunt, Dad, and in the process I have collected so, *so* much along the way.

Earlier this evening, I began flipping through the pages of this journal, this *journey.* Take all this in the humblest way possible ... but it's amazing to watch how much I've grown. Yes, I'm more worldly, well-traveled, and capable, but the changes run much deeper than those superficial improvements. I'm also more self-possessed. I'm more patient, more relaxed, and yet also more determined and convicted. I'm more hopeful and less anxious. My empathy has grown and my selfishness withered. I can better discern between what's important and what's trivial, what's genuine and what's flashy. Even in my day-by-day writing, I can practically watch an evolution, a metamorphosis, happening right before my very eyes. No longer am I the college girl who felt she had to guard herself with machismo and cynicism, even when writing to her long-gone father in a diary. I've become someone else entirely, a woman who is unafraid of her story and unashamed to tell that story to anyone who needs it.

I have already mined my ton of gold from this adventure. And not just the treasures you've led me to find, Dad. Also the nuggets I've dug up and discovered for *myself.* If I'm lucky enough to add to my hoard by finding your final letter, I'll be all the richer for it. But if not, I'll leave Iceland content, recognizing and appreciating the new wealth that's already mine.

Two days, Dad. That's all I'm giving you. For now, at least. I know you wanted me to press on for a month if necessary. I'm giving you two more days. Then I'll leave with Mom to enjoy the gift of life I have, now enriched by all my new treasures. I'm not saying I wouldn't come back someday to try again ... but two days is all I'm promising.

So, if you really care about me finishing your scavenger hunt, you'd better send an angel to guide my way. Preferably one with a better compass than this piece of crap you left me.

Love, your (filthy rich) little girl,
Kate

EIGHT

The Final Piece

August 7, 2023

Dear Dad,

I see you got my note about the angel.

I also see that your plans, while well-guarded against failure, weren't bulletproof. Fortunately, Lady Luck must have the hots for you, because she constantly seems to have your back. Whether she ends up saving your ass here remains to be seen.

After yet another fruitless day in vain pursuit of your letter, Mom and I were finishing our dinner at the inn restaurant. Since there was no one else eating right then, the owner, an older man named Einar who basically runs the whole place, sidled up to chat with us.

"Most tourists," he said, parking a chair next to our table and sitting with a creaky sigh, "only are here a night or two. They see the cliffs, and they move on. This is your fifth night. Why stay so long?"

His tone was friendly, his gentle aura the kind which invites immediate trust, so I shared the long version of the story. When I arrived at the chapter about our present predicament, he clucked his tongue and chuckled softly.

"It appears your father forgot something in his plans," Einar said. "*North* back in 2003 is not the same *north* as it is today in 2023."

Mom and I exchanged quizzical glances before I asked, "What do you mean? North is north, isn't it?"

"On a map or a globe, yes," Einar answered. "But, in truth, there are *two* norths. There is geographic north, the top of the globe. That never changes. Then there is also magnetic north, the pole of Earth's magnetic field. When you use a compass, the needle points to magnetic north, not geographic. What your father failed to realize is that magnetic north is always changing, drifting from place to place. In recent years it has moved at an exceptional rate. To put it simply, you've been following the wrong heading from your starting point at the cliff top."

I was floored. So was Mom. For days we'd been following a false trail. A fierce clenching in my gut accompanied the revelation.

"So there's no way to find it," I muttered matter-of-factly. "It's lost, unless I wander around forever and hope I get lucky."

The corners of Einar's eyes crinkled with a grin, and he scoffed. "I will never understand you young people! You do nothing but play with the Internet all day long. Then, the moment you actually *need* it for something, you forget it exists!"

"What do you mean?" I wondered.

"I mean," he said, "that you can find anything on Google if you look hard enough. That includes the position of magnetic north in 2003."

"Yeah, but my compass doesn't know that," I protested, offended at his condescension. "It's still going to point to 2023's north pole."

Einar raised a gnarled and leathery hand in a gesture of peace. He replied, "I can help you with that. It is only a matter of learning the difference in angle between the two norths. Then you follow that margin of difference from the north of your compass needle."

"Can you show me how?" I asked. A sudden vigor had conquered the doldrums of my defeat.

"I can. Tomorrow, after breakfast."

Sooooooo once again, I'm too excited to sleep. The end of the trail is almost beneath my feet, your last letter so close I can already feel it in my hands. It's strange, but I'm worried I might be let down. In my head I've built up how deep, profound, impactful, *life-changing* those final words must be. Somehow, it seems impossible that anything you say could live up to my lofty expectations.

Oh well. You haven't let me down yet, right? I guess there's no reason I should be afraid you'll start now.

OK ... Mom's already asleep in the bed next to mine. I should probably shut off my light and try to get some rest.

Love, your (treasure-bound) little girl,
Kate

DEAR KATE—

A picture is worth a thousand words.

August 8, 2023

Dear Dad,

Five or six years ago, Mom told me about something that happened after you died. It was one of the few stories she managed to share with me through her sadness, even so many years after you left. She said that, in the days after you died, I'd be toddling around the house. Each time I came across a picture of you, I would strike a giant grin and exclaim, "Dada! Dada!" It was like I finally found where you'd been hiding so long. Whenever it happened, she said she would break down in tears. Eventually, she put away all the pictures of you, because each time it was like you were dying all over again.

Today I was the one sobbing as I stared down at photographs from the distant past.

You tricked me, you know. Maybe you realized you had to throw a change-up into the mix. Something unpredictable. Something so vastly different from my highest expectations that it would make disappointment impossible.

When I opened that buried metal lockbox (as well as the subsequent half-dozen plastic bags) and pulled out the envelope, I recognized right away there was something different about it. The thickness wasn't uniform from end to end. It was lumpy, not flat and smooth like a letter. Carefully, I unsealed the envelope and slid my fingers inside.

When I withdrew its contents, my heart broke.

Mom gasped, then laughed, then whispered, "So *that's* where they've been. All this time! Isaac Jackson ... you crazy, wonderful, beautiful man."

One by one, I flipped through the pictures, photographs you took with the same Polaroid camera currently buried in my backpack. *Your* backpack. When I was done, I sorted through them again, more deliberately, savoring them, so I could soak in every smile, every shimmering gleam in your brown eyes, every streak of color in your face and clothes and hands and hair, every lumen of radiant joy beaming from every inch of you.

Eight pictures. That's all you needed. Eight palm-sized Polaroids to tell your final story.

There, in the first grainy photo, is a sleeping blonde bundle, no more than ten pounds, nestled in perfect safety between the strong, moonlit arms of her Dada. He beams down upon her, and not even nighttime's shadowy cloak can extinguish the light of amazement in his tired eyes as he rocks and dreams about life with his little girl.

The second one is also marred by the blur of darkness. Now the girl is older. A knit, woolen winter cap is constricting her head and hiding half her face. A blanket of gray snow covers the lower half of the image, black sky the upper. Snaking from end to end are the faintest tendrils of emerald and crimson. They are the northern lights. As the small girl stares, captivated, up into heaven, the man holding her is held captive by something else: the pudgy child herself. He cannot look away, not even for a moment, for fear he might miss a single breath.

Colors pop in the brilliant sunshine. Photo #3 is much clearer, illuminated not by northern lights but by azure and unclouded skies. In the background is a milky sapphire lake, crowned by triple spires of granite. The crystal-blue irises of that same blond kid are clear now as she grins into the camera. The dark-featured man posing next to her is glancing sideways, not at the lens but at his daughter. He is a towering figure beside her infant frame. A protector watching over her forever.

The man in the next picture is the same ... yet different. His scraggly beard attempts to cover up how thin he has become. His shoulders, once chiseled as with an axe, are withered, and his arms wispy. Sitting on his knee, one hand stroking the wild beard, is the girl. Only a few months have transformed her from baby to toddler. Now she has a full head of hair. Behind them the frosted caps of the Alaska Range stare down, inviting them to partake in adventure and exploration. But the man is oblivious. Again, he has eyes only for the girl.

The scene changes. Now father and daughter sit, side by side, backs to the camera, on a sun-bleached log. The child stares at the sunset far across the pebbled beach. The father stares at her, his eyes crinkled at the corners as his gaunt lips grin, content. His expression is of pure, concentrated wonder, as if he could watch his daughter, unblinking, for the next hundred years.

The sixth picture has as its backdrop a multihued sea of red and beige tile. The girl stands on top of Lucca's great wall. Behind her the man is crouching, his hands around her tiny shoulders. Her flowered dress is frozen, mid-billow, tugged aside by the Tuscan breeze along with her stringy hair, all of it caught and immortalized by the camera's shutter. The same love bleeds from the man's eyes, which are transfixed—*always* transfixed—on the girl. Now, though, pain is also present in his gaze. He knows his time with her is almost up. Soon it will consume the final moments of his life, and he will forever be separated from his little girl.

I flipped to the next photo. The seventh. Taken along the edge of the very same cliffs I've been visiting for five days. In this one the man has mustered all his strength. With heroic effort he holds his daughter high above his head. Her arms, legs, are raised and straight. She is flying. Her Dada is her wind. The pain, at least for today, is gone from his eyes. Only purest joy emanates upward at his daughter as she sails upon the sky.

My first time thumbing through the pictures, I assumed this seventh photo would be the final one. After all, these bird cliffs were the last stop on your little scavenger hunt. I was wrong. There is an eighth.

It's the only one you labeled, Dad. Scrawled upon the white margin above the picture, in a hand I find all too familiar, are the words: *My Favorite Place on Earth.* Below them is me, sleeping in the turquoise-framed toddler bed I used as a child. The stuffed, blue pony hugged tight in my pudgy arms still sits on my bed to this very day, and the room is the one I continue to call my own even as a college girl. The only thing missing between the picture and the present is the skeleton-thin man curled uncomfortably next to me on the bed, holding my hand in his own, fast asleep.

And in the narrow, blank space at the bottom of the Polaroid, spelled out like the epitaph on a gravestone, are the last words I will ever hear from you:

I LOVE YOU. NOW AND ALWAYS.
DAD

In the end, there was no lesson. No final bit of wisdom to leave with me. Just the story of a father's love—your love—for his daughter to watch unfold before her very own tear-soaked eyes.

You led me here. In those final days of your sickness, you poured all your energy, all your time, and all your heart into this last incredible love letter. All for a daughter too young to have any memory of you. So she could see that you were always with her. And that you always will be.

No treasure is greater than this. No one is richer than I am.

Thank you, Dada, for spending yourself so that I would know this story.

Love, your (now and always) little girl,
Kate

August 17, 2023

Dear Dad,

The last week-and-change have gone by in a hazy blur. Mom and I are back in Colorado now. Bit by bit during that time, it's like she's been fitting pieces into a puzzle to complete the whole picture. Pieces she never realized she had, but which she has carried all along. Or maybe it would be more accurate to say that she never knew which puzzle they belonged to until now.

Of course, during the last months of your life, it didn't surprise her that you wanted to revisit some of the places you'd always loved the most. She also knew about the letters you were planting for me to find when I was 21. Wherever you had traveled in life, she said you always took your Polaroid camera along. That's why she didn't think anything of it when you wanted pictures with me at the various locations we visited. She also detected nothing strange when you wanted to take me to Iceland on a father-daughter-*only* trip.

"He was always sentimental about you," she said, "even before he got sick. I thought it was a sweet idea."

It wasn't until months after you died, when Mom was going through your old photos, that she realized some pictures were missing—including the secret one she had taken of us sleeping in my bed. By that time she had stopped thinking about the scavenger hunt you assembled, so the notion never crossed her mind that those photos might be the pot of gold at the end of your rainbow. You had given her access to every other part of the game.

Just not the final play.

"He did it like that because he knew it would impress me one last time," she theorized at dinner a couple nights ago. "That stupid, sweet man was always trying to impress me. I have to admit, it worked!"

So, Mom's impressed. Almost euphoric these days, actually. Nice job.

But I'm not sure where my heart is. Mom's been sharing the story with anyone who will listen, from her siblings to the grocery store produce dude. Other than Franco and Emma, however, I haven't told a soul.

Now that the game is over, do you know what I've been doing? I've been lying in bed, alternating between your pictures and your letters. I'm a sheep chewing its cud as I spend hours ruminating over everything that's happened in the past months, over how much you've altered my course, my entire outlook on everything. Assessing where I am and wondering where I should go.

I suppose I should have expected this. After the exhilaration of reaching a mountain peak, there always comes the inevitable and tiresome trip back down. That's just how life works. For me, the victory and closure I tasted in Iceland are now being followed by a descent back to level ground. I don't know if I'd say I'm in a funk exactly, but every night when I should be sleeping, I keep asking myself the same questions: "What's my next mountain? Where do I go from here?"

For the moment at least, I'm answerless. Thanks a lot, Dad. (I'm back to being angry at you, by the way. Before you showed up again, I was perfectly happy taking the easy road through life. A girl isn't tortured with all these annoying, soul-searching kinds of questions when she's complacent and too naïve to know any better.)

I guess I do have *one* answer among all the many questions: I know my life can't go back to what it was before. That's why, this morning, I called the

Wyoming admissions office to tell them I'm taking a hiatus from school this fall. I may not know what the answer is, but I am absolutely sure it has nothing to do with a career as an actuary. I'll be damned if I'm gonna spend my life sitting in any kind of office.

In the meantime, I'll wait. I'll think. I'll keep my eyes a lot more open than in my previous 21 years. I'll travel. I'll climb mountains. I'll do some good. I'll remember you. And I'll miss you.

Mostly, though, I'll make the most of the time I have—however long that time might be—to love people as hard as I can and to love life the way my Dad did.

In the end, the rest is just details. Whatever they are, if I approach life the way you taught me, those details will be good.

But my journal is running out of pages. There may still be an important moment or two worth sharing before those pages are gone, so I better shut up now and save them. I don't know how long it will be before I write to you again. Until I do, keep enjoying yourself up there!

And, if you can spare a moment now and then, keep an eye on me too.

Love, your (delightfully aimless) little girl,
Kate

---------- EPILOGUE ----------

It Ends with an Epitaph

December 25, 2023

Dear Dad,

It's hard to believe one full year has passed since the night I read your first letter. Somehow it seems both too long *and* too short. Too long because so much has happened in between. Everything has changed since that fate-filled night. Too short because ... well, because that's just how life seems to work.

You know, people talk about *life changes* all the time. "Kids are such a major life change." "Switching careers? What a huge life change you've got goin' on!" But I went through so many in the past year that I'm left wondering whether they're as rare and noteworthy as people think.

I'm not just talking about all the personal character transformations you forced me into. There was also the change in my career path. I was on the fast track to calculating risk assessment before your little intervention. Now I'm enrolled to begin a journalism major at the University of Northern Colorado up in Greeley. Plus, I pitched a piece to your old magazine about the scavenger hunt you sent me on. They told me it was too lengthy for a single issue. That's why they'll be publishing it in eight parts over the next few months. For a first-timer in the cutthroat world of freelance journalism, I'm told they paid pretty handsomely for your story! It's my dream now to follow in your footsteps, to become a storyteller myself, so that I can share the myriad tales of people and places across the globe.

Of course, we can't forget the change in my romantic objects. Just 364 days ago, I was sitting in front of a fireplace with Andrew, trying to avoid a conversation about the future as resolutely as Willie Nelson a barbershop. Now Andrew is married, and I spent Christmas doing shots with my Patagonian prince.

That's right, Franco is here! It was a complete surprise (to me) when he showed up at our house this morning. He's been telling me for weeks he'd be stuck working, but it turns out he and Mom have been in cahoots for over a month planning this little Christmas miracle for me. Then, to add to the surprise, he informed me that he's leaving his municipal job in Arica. He received his green card and in one week will be an official employee of the Colorado State Parks Department! He already has an apartment in Lyons, about half an hour from here. It's a pretty serious move on his part. A year ago, a very different me might have run for the foothills.

But not now. Not with him. I think it's perfect, and I couldn't be happier about it.

This next change might be a tough one for you to hear, Dad, so I hope you're sitting down. Or doing whatever it is you dead folks do when you're about to receive shocking news.

Ready? Here goes ...

Gary proposed to Mom at Thanksgiving. She said yes. I'm sure I saw her happier with you when I was an infant, but since I have no actual memories of that time, I have to say, this is the happiest I can ever *remember* seeing her.

Before you throw a tantrum or work some spirit voodoo to haunt them and curse their marriage, you should know that Gary really loves Mom. He treats her with all the kindness and respect she deserves. I hate to say it, but you should probably find a way to thank the guy. He has brought the woman you love a light heart and zest for life that she hasn't shown in a coon's age.

They're getting married at the end of January. I know it's kind of quick, but if there's any way for you to attend, I think you should.

And that segues into the final life change ...

Mom is selling the house and moving into Gary's. I was sad at first. I even cried. After all, this is the only home I've ever known. It's the only house I ever lived in with you.

But in the end, I knew it had to be like this. The world moves on, and we little people have to move on with it. Remembering the beauty (and the pain) of the past is good for us. Through it, we learn many of the most important lessons life has to give. But *clinging* to the past? Holding on and trying to live in it? That's disaster, a spiritual suicide which leaves the body alive without the person truly *being* alive.

For a long time, almost my whole life, that was Mom. Alive, yet not fully so. She was chained to all the memories of you that dwell in this house. She never could quite escape. And as long as she stays here, she'll never find complete freedom.

That's why she has to leave.

I, on the other hand, have to leave because I'm guessing the new owners won't buy my Squatter's Rights argument as a reason to let me stay. Already the boxes are piling up along the walls of my room and on top of your old writing desk. Soon they'll all move with me to Emma's and my new apartment in Greeley. (She decided to get a degree after all. Go her! Long story. Anyway ...)

A chapter ends. A chapter begins. Our stories go on, until the day they don't anymore.

You know what I'm talking about even better than I do.

Anyway, I thought you should know about all this major stuff going down. Figured it was worth a few pages!

Merry Christmas to you, Dad.

And a happy 22nd birthday to me!

Love, your (in transit) little girl,
Kate

June 7, 2025

Dear Dad,

Just as when I wrote so long ago, there still aren't many days when I walk around with the sense that I've been jilted or cheated over losing you. Today, however, I did—and worse than ever before. Since this also takes the prize for "Happiest Day of My Life," today truly was a recipe for a wedding cake of mixed emotions.

Don't get me wrong, I love Uncle Ben to pieces. But it's supposed to be a father who walks his little girl down the aisle. Even Mom had that pleasure for the *second* time when she married Gary.

But you were gone long before I even knew what marriage was. So yeah, I felt a little cheated today. To be honest, you were as much on my mind during the ceremony as the man standing next to me. I found myself silently praying, pleading to heaven again and again, that they might let you out for a few minutes so you could watch my wedding and bless my marriage.

We spoke our "I do's." Franco kissed his bride. We paraded out the back of the quaint mountain church and into the brilliant daylight waiting beyond the double doors. I happened then to glance up at the sky, and even though the afternoon sun still burned brightly above us, I saw something else overhead.

A thin, distinct ribbon of light, draped across the heavens.

I nudged Franco and pointed, but by the time he turned his attention from Emma and Patagonian Ranger Paulo, the beaming bridal party twosome following us, the light had shimmered and disappeared.

"What is it?" he asked with distracted confusion.

"It's ... nothing," I replied, giving a slight shrug and shake of the head. Then I grinned, showing him all of my recently whitened teeth, and kissed him again like I was kissing him for the first time.

Maybe it was nothing, that thread of celestial light. Maybe it was only a girl's foolish hope planting a false and momentary vision in my head. But during that fleeting frame on time's eternal reel, I had absolute conviction. It was Bivrost, the "shaking road" of the Norsemen, connecting heaven to earth, so that the long-gone father at its other end could watch over his little girl on her wedding day.

Speaking of wedding days, I should probably get going. Franco has gotten used to my uncompromising and abrupt compulsion to drop everything and write my thoughts before I lose them, but at the moment he looks rather murderous, glowering at me from the bed of our newlywed suite. I guess I should give him some attention.

Can't say I blame him. I look damn good in this dress.

Love, your (married!) little girl,
Kate

March 19, 2028

Dear Dad,

I thought I understood you. The letters. The pictures. All those years ago as I stood atop the Bird Cliffs, I was sure I knew your heart completely.

The truth was, though, that even then I only saw a sliver. I was a child catching a fleeting glimpse of a magnificent work of art behind a fluttering curtain. You did your best through your words and with your photographs, but there were certain parts of your heart, of a father's love, that were bound to remain hidden to a child like me, no matter how hard you tried to show me.

So you see, the 21-year-old, college-girl Kate didn't stand a chance.

The Kate who became a mom at 4:02 this morning? She gets it. She sees.

Because the moment that nurse laid your grandson in my arms, your heart became my heart. The same bonds that tied you forever to me are the ones which now bind me to my baby boy. And nothing—not even death or hell itself—will sever those chains or tear my heart away from him.

Even though I have only seen the tiniest sliver of his life, I already know, without any doubt, that he will always be my joy. My treasure. The wonder of my living, beating heart.

Just as I was yours. And just as I always will be.

Wherever you are, Dad, whatever you're doing, however far away you might be, I hope you can take even one moment to see and say hello to this beautiful, brown-haired boy snuggling and sleeping in the crook of my arm.

You won't be disappointed. I promise.

Love, your (exhausted, exhilarated) little girl,
Kate

December 25, 2032

Dear Dada,

When I was still in college, I thought it was childish, even foolish, to address you like a child would. Now that I'm grown, and a twice-over mom myself, I can't imagine calling you anything else. You're my Dada. You always were my Dada, and you always will be.

Something always seems to be staining my fingertips these days. Usually the purple ink of my favorite fountain pen is the culprit. If not that, it's watercolor or marker or blueberry juice or whatever else my kids and I are playing with that particular day. This warm Christmas afternoon, it happens to be Colorado dirt caked beneath my fingernails, turning the skin around them a dusty, aged sort of yellow.

In front of me is a shallow grave, unfilled. I dug it only moments ago, on top of another one. On top of *your* grave, Dada.

You know, ever since your letters, I've never visited this place. Maybe it's because I could finally understand—and mourn over—everything I lost when I lost you. Or maybe it's because your letters made you feel, for a time, so real to me. So *alive.* Whatever the reason, I wasn't able to do it. To confront you as you are now. Resting in peace six feet below me, your incredible life commemorated by a cold, weathered, lifeless gravestone.

Now that I'm here, I realize there was nothing to fear all along. You remain as alive in my heart and mind as ever. So real, I feel I could almost touch you. Talk to you. Embrace you.

It's actually quite peaceful here. If you could see it, I think you would like it. A brisk, scented breeze sweeps down from the mountains. Overhead, the whispering leaves of the aspen provide you with plenty of shade any time of day. And on this day at least, no one else is here. All is quiet.

Except, of course, for your grandchildren climbing a tree only a stone's throw from here. Isaac, my intrepid boy, is about ten feet off the ground now. (That's right, I named him after you. One final cliché, naming him after his dead grandpa.) He's fearless. Bold. Like his parents. Like you.

His little sister, Abbie, leans more toward caution. I don't know where she inherited that trait, but it currently has her two-year-old ass sitting on the lowest branch about thirty inches off the ground. Every day I watch over them, guarding them, protecting them, as my mother and father did for me.

Those beautiful children—and their dad—are my life. I don't know where I'd be without them. Every time I look at their faces, I thank God for sewing them into the fabric of my world.

And, Dad, I thank you. Call it an unintended consequence of your scavenger hunt. Or, if you prefer, call it an inexplicable premonition spoken by Fate through your letters. In the end, it doesn't matter *how* it all happened. What matters is that it *did* happen.

Because of you.

You gave me my husband. You gave me a career that fills me with a sense of passion and purpose every single day. You gave me those two amazing children in the tree.

You gave me my life, Dada. You gave me my *home* in the truest sense of the word.

Today, it's time for me to give something back. To inscribe a secret epitaph upon the hallowed ground of your final resting place.

That's what brings us here, to this freshly excavated hole in the ground. Thirty years have passed since the first burial in this cemetery plot. Now it's time for one more. Too long I've put it off. I didn't want the days of the diary to come to their end. I didn't want our adventure together to be over.

But here we are. We've arrived at the finish line, Dad. The final pages. The last words I'll ever write to you. It seems fitting, I suppose, doing this today. After all, this sunny Christmas afternoon marks ten years. Ten exhausting, thrilling, toilsome, exquisite, challenging, wonder-filled years since the night of your first letter to me ... and mine to you.

The metal lockbox you buried in Iceland is waiting on the ground next to me. I figured it would serve as a poetic coffin, returned to the man who first buried it above the bird cliffs. When the ink of my final letter is dry, I'll seal this book in plastic, then in the box, and then within the earth itself. I suppose our story will stay there, committed to your safekeeping until the end of days. (Or at least until a grave robber comes for you.)

But the journal will not be alone. Yes, I have written thousands of words to you. Words, though, are only worth so much. A picture, on the other hand, is worth a thousand of them. If words are the puzzle pieces of the heart, then pictures are an album. You, in your oh-so-clever way, taught me that.

It is, admittedly, a little hard for me to part with these photographs. I snapped them with your Polaroid camera, which means only one of each exists. But I think you need them more than I do. After all, every day the faces in these pictures are the ones I hold in my hands. At any time I can book a flight to explore these breathtaking landscapes. You can't.

That's why I need you to have them. So you can see, with your own eyes and for all eternity, the life you gave me.

Here is Isaac: at the hospital when he was born; at the hospital again when he swelled up like a Sumo after trying peanuts the first time; blowing out the chunky #2 candle on his Curious George birthday cake; nestled in my arms as we rock, back and forth, in the same chair and on the same porch where, ages ago, you comforted my infant self.

Here is Abbie: sleeping in her car seat on a trip to Nana's house; scooting around our driveway on her foot bike; teetering a bit too close for her dad's comfort on the edge of the Látrabjarg bird cliffs. (Franco is softer than McDonald's ice cream in July when it comes to her. I think you can relate.)

And there's Mom: gazing out at a Tuscan sunset from the walls of Lucca on our mother-daughter trip last year; blowing out the fifty candles on her birthday cake; playing with Abbie in the pool at a family reunion; sleeping on the sofa with one grandkid tucked beneath each arm.

Of course, there are also plenty of me: wearing my wedding gown; sitting at my new desk on my first day working for *Beyond Outdoor* magazine; bathing in a Thai jungle pool with my arm around Emma; hiking in the Tetons; standing in front of Cinderella's Castle at Disney; arm in arm with Franco in front of our newly purchased home, a mountain paradise sold to us by none other than Grandpa himself shortly before he passed. I hope it doesn't come across as narcissism, but most of the pictures going into the box are of me. Somehow, after everything, I figure those are the ones you'll be most anxious to see.

But I think the photos you'll enjoy best are the Polaroids I took during my twenty-first year.

Because that was the year I spent with my Dada.

There are exactly seven of them. Seven pictures of your Kate, your all-grown-up Cuddles, as we journeyed around the world together.

Your face may not appear in any of them. But you were always there. You were always right beside me.

You know, Dad, when I was growing up, people kept telling me you died too young. I used to agree. Now I think it's bullshit. That's an expression people use when someone passes away before they've had much opportunity to experience life or leave their footprint on this world.

But you did both. You didn't simply endure your life, as so many do. You really, truly, *lived* it.

And, while no one will ever write about you in any history book, these pictures are the ironclad proof that your footprint on this earth, and in my life, is nothing short of magnificent.

I love you now and always,
Kate

DENALI MAJESTO
HONOR SEQUITUR FUGIENTEM

www.ingramcontent.com/pod-product-compliance
Lightning Source LLC
Chambersburg PA
CBHW010713020826
48980CB00023B/973/J

* 9 7 9 8 9 9 2 8 0 3 8 2 2 *